DARK ENOUGH TO DANCE

Also by Colin Hayward:

Other Times, Other Places: Twenty Stories
Scrivener Press, 2006

To John
Best
Wishes
Colin

DARK

ENOUGH TO

DANCE

Two Short Stories and Two Novellas

BY

COLIN HAYWARD

Scrivener Press

Library and Archives Canada Cataloguing in Publication

Hayward, Colin, 1942-, author
    Dark enough to dance : two short stories and two novellas / by Colin Hayward.

ISBN 978-1-896350-62-2 (pbk.)

    I. Title.

PS8615.A885D37 2013   C813'.6   C2013-905314-X

Book design: Laurence Steven
Cover design: Linda Hayward
Photo of author: Linda Hayward
Chapter photos: Colin and Linda Hayward

Published by Scrivener Press
465 Loach's Road,
Sudbury, Ontario, Canada, P3E 2R2
info@yourscrivenerpress.com
www.scrivenerpress.com

We acknowledge the financial support of the Canada Council for the Arts and the Ontario Arts Council for our publishing activities.

Dedicated to
the travelling
Escudos Committee

SPECIAL THANKS

to

Gary Bouchard, Marti Carding, Rick Cooper, Judy Duncan,
Mike Eadie, Anadel Hastie, Linda Hayward, Don Lake,
Nigel Leith, Jeannette Mallay, Diane McLean, Jose Antonio
Hernandez Roderiguez, Mike Steinman, Paula Wharton

TABLE OF CONTENTS

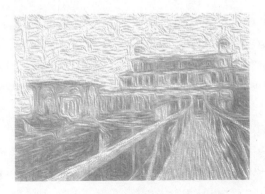

THE INVISIBLE WOMAN

Three days of incessant rain. Eleanor was sure that she had never ever seen rain like this back in Canada. Stupid to come to England in November to see where her parents had come from. Mind you, the timing had not been hers. Oh, no. Her teaching career had ended at exactly 2:16 p.m. October 28th. She knew the exact time because, after she had slapped Ashley Terrence-Hartley across the face, she had stared at the clock at the back of the classroom, unable to look at the class in case she burst into tears.

A collective gasp from her grade eleven class had been followed by the slamming of the door as Ashley had rushed out into the hall on her way, no doubt, to the office.

"She had been complaining about her mark again," Eleanor had explained to the principal. "I told her that the mark was correct. Then Ashley had muttered something as she turned away. Several of the girls in front had started snickering. I said, 'Wait a minute. Come back here' which she did with an odd look on her face. I asked her what she had just said. She just sneered and said, 'You wouldn't want to know.' 'Then you are to stand here until you tell me,' I said. 'I just said that you were pathetic. Now can I go and sit down?' And that's when I slapped her face."

"Her parents have already called demanding your dismissal," said the principal. "It's a very serious charge. Striking a child."

Eleanor had shaken her head. This was what she got after twenty…no, twenty-one years of teaching at St. Elizabeth Bichier's Academy for Girls. Everybody knew that many of the girls, like Ashley, were students here because they had worn out their welcome at more than one public high school. "She called me 'pathetic'!" Eleanor protested.

The principal turned towards the window behind her desk and said, "An apology might help but I can't promise anything."

"She'll get no apology from me. If anything, she's the one that owes me an apology."

Her enforced leave had ended in termination. Eleanor had cried a lot the day she received the notice but by that evening, the tears had dried. Making herself a cup of tea, she told herself, "You never liked teaching much anyway. Remember how depressed you got every Labour Day at the prospect of facing them again. Some years you'd even throw up on the first day of school." She shook her head but then managed a smile. "I'm going to travel." Where? To Brighton on the south coast of England, the place her parents had met before emigrating to Canada and having her.

After her dismissal, no one called. For the two and a half weeks before her departure, the only voice that did not emanate from the television or CBC radio was her own.

One night after brushing her teeth, she looked at herself

in the mirror. A plain woman in her early fifties looked back. 'Nondescript' was the word that sprang to mind.

Even when she went out shopping, no one seemed to notice her. A couple of times she saw people she knew but they would hurry past as if they had not seen her.

The night before she left for England, she looked critically at herself in the mirror again. Maybe it's the light, she thought, but I seem to be fading. She wiped the mirror with the face cloth in case there had been some steam clouding her image. But no. A moment of panic before she scrambled out into the hall.

At the airport, security was much more concerned about what was in her purse and pockets than in her.

After landing at Heathrow, she had taken the train down to Brighton and checked into a hotel overlooking the sea. Her room was on the fourth floor so she could see a large stretch of pebble beach and, to her right, the West Pier. Some British movie had been shot there but she could not remember the name.

And almost as soon as she arrived, Eleanor had realized that she had no idea where in Brighton her parents had lived. So there was really no reason to be here, off season at a seaside resort in the rain where few tourists had appeared over the past three days. Driven by constant winds, the rains washed in sheets across King's Road, the wide street running along the seawall below her. The sea constantly hammered the beach, waves crashing in and then receding with a watery rattle as they clawed at the pebbles, dragging them back into the roil of the surf.

She had stayed in her room even though it was so constantly cold, despite the clanking of the old radiator, that she wore most of her clothes, even to bed.

The discolored mirror in the bathroom confirmed her

worst fears. She seemed to have faded even more since leaving home. The edges of her face had become indistinct. Her graying hair seemed as insubstantial as smoke. Even her eye colour was fading, becoming dull, muddy.

She had run out of the bathroom and cowered in the queen-sized bed, the covers pulled up to her nose. "Maybe it's your eyes," she told herself. Feeling slightly foolish, she covered one eye and focused on the transom over the door. It seemed clear. Same with the other. She put on her glasses and picked up a book from the bedside table. Both eyes seemed to be fine.

That night she left the light on as if that would make her more visible. Even so she hardly slept.

In the morning, she went down to the all-but-deserted dining room and helped herself to a cup of tea, some cold toast and congealed scrambled eggs from the buffet.

With something in her stomach, she felt a little better. She stood at the window. Yesterday's rain had been replaced by a low fog rolling in from the sea. She looked over towards the West Pier but all she could see of it was the cupola over the bandstand poking above the low lying fog. *Oh! What a Lovely War.* That had been the movie they had filmed on the West Pier. Below her, only the tops of the streetlights were still visible. Still, the rain had finally stopped, so she resolved to dress as warmly as she could and walk over towards the old pier.

But first, she had had an idea at breakfast. Rummaging through her suitcase, she uncovered her old Polaroid camera. God knew how much longer they were going to make film for it. Should have bought a new camera before she left. In fact, she had only thought of bringing a camera of any sort at the last minute and shoved in the Polaroid sx-70 given to her by her father. Never mind. It would have to do.

With a couple of her books, she propped the camera up in front of the dresser mirror so that it would take a picture of her reflection. After the first shot, she waved the blank Polaroid to hurry its drying process and then stared at it as the image began to crystallize. This process had always thrilled her, the magical appearance of a moment in time. As the image struggled out of the black rectangle, her jaw dropped. The wall behind her was there, but no sign of her own image. She adjusted the angle over and over, getting more and more frantic. By the time she was out of film there were Polaroids all over the dresser and the floor.

Getting up, she looked around for her coat and plastic rain hat, put them on and almost ran to the lift.

Out on the street, she pulled up her collar and set out towards the West Pier, feeling as if she was watching herself from the window of her room, watching herself disappear into the fog.

She made slow progress. Occasionally, the headlights of a car would flare in front of her, looming into sight like a sketch moving in slow motion before fading to two tiny red dots and winking out. Just as she was beginning to think that she had passed the pier, the outline of its wrought iron traceries loomed to her left.

The West Pier, jutting out into the Atlantic, had seen better days. There had even been talk of closing it because it was unsafe. Eleanor liked its air of faded gentility, its Victorian wrought iron filigree and wooden benches. Her parents had almost certainly come here in its heyday. Hurrying past Madame Rosa's fortune teller booth, now closed, a memory stopped her. "A fortune teller once told me, I would move far away and have a girl," her mother had said more than once. This had to be the place. The thought cheered her a little.

She found a bench out of the wind and sat down. Just visible, the curling surf racing past was thrilling. From time to time, a particularly fierce wave would pound the pier and she would feel it shudder. After a while, she was so cold and stiff that she wrapped her arms around herself and rocked on the hard slats.

Imperceptibly, the fog had thickened since she had sat down. She realized this when she noticed that the iron handrails had faded from view. In a moment of panic, she got to her feet, took two steps, turned around and became disoriented. With her arms thrust out in front of her, she shuffled ahead until she touched something solid: a wrought iron column. Her heart pounding, she clung to it desperately.

Beneath her feet the worn boards vibrated to the rhythm of the waves like the engine of a tramp steamer carrying its invisible cargo out into the vast ocean beyond. Above the fog Eleanor could hear the muffled keening of the gulls slowly fading away.

DANZA PARA TRES

Connor had been in Cuba for more than a week before Zoe discovered that he had left the Sudbury area. Yesterday a major snowstorm had dumped twenty centimetres but today the temperature had dropped to –28° Celsius, and the roads were clear. The sun was shining again and Zoe wore sunglasses against the brittle winter light reflecting off the banks of snow. Driving to the airport to pick up Aden took Zoe past Connor's house. She was surprised to see his vehicle was buried in snow that had obliterated the driveway. A meter-high drift from the plough had choked the entrance. Maybe he's sick. She thought of stopping but she was already late for the plane and Aden's temper these days was not of the best. As it turned out, the Dash-8 coming in from Toronto had been delayed for an hour and a half so she need not have hurried. Rather than sit around the airport, Zoe returned to her car. At least she could have a cigarette there.

Zoe had started smoking, like many dancers, when she

was a teenager as a way to control her appetite and, although she had tried to quit several times, she had been unable to shake the habit. "It calms me," she told anyone who asked why she still smoked despite the risks. She would rarely admit that she really enjoyed the little rituals that smoking involved. As she lit her first cigarette in a couple of hours, she felt the slight thrill of the nicotine hit and thought of Connor. An hour and a half. She had time to drive back and check on the house, only five minutes down the road. Better than sitting here. She started her car and drove back down the hill. At the T-junction, she turned left, and passed Freskiw's, the plant sellers, long since closed for the winter. At the mouth of Connor's driveway she stopped the car, got out and looked at the house. She could not identify precisely why but even from here the house felt empty, deserted.

A transport roared by, blasting her with a rush of frigid air; she began to climb the bank into the clogged driveway. By the time she reached the front door her boots were full of snow. She knocked and rang the bell, even peered in the living room window. No sign of life. She was about to leave when she remembered the spare key. Did he still keep it in the dead birch? Worth a look. She was already wet. She trudged across the drifts on the lawn to the path through the trees. Sure enough, the key was wedged into the same ancient woodpecker hole.

Kicking away the snow that had accumulated in front of the door, she let herself in. The house was cold so she kept her coat on. Feeling unsettled, she called Connor's name a couple of times. A scurrying sound made her jump but otherwise the place was silent. She was reluctant to go any farther in, afraid of what she might find. She had been thinking about him more and more during the past couple of months and now she felt guilty that she had not kept in touch. He should not have been living alone with his asthma.

Mustering her courage, she slowly climbed the few stairs to the main floor and looked around. The kitchen was unusually tidy but that was all. She went down the hall, steeled herself and looked into what had been their bedroom. Empty. She sighed with relief as she backtracked to the kitchen. The daylight was fading and she switched on a light. Nothing. She tried the phone. Dead. The gas fire downstairs must still be on because, although it was cool in the house, she could not see her breath.

He's really gone, she realized, feeling a well of conflicting emotions. Didn't even call to say goodbye. She sank on to a kitchen chair, surprised at how upset she felt. Gone.

Connor had not been in touch since the divorce. Oh, Zoe knew how hurt he had been when she had moved in with Aden but it had been the combination of Aden's jealousy and the finality of the divorce that had erected the barrier between them.

Zoe pulled out a cigarette and was about to rise and step out on the deck behind the house when she realized that she no longer needed to smoke outside. Inhaling deeply, she got up and began to look through the house. She knew there was no time to lose as the winter sun was descending beyond the rock ridge to the west and soon the light would be gone. In the bedroom, she found a copy of *The Sun Also Rises* on the bedside table. Hemingway. Connor had read most of Hemingway's works after their trip to Cuba. Is that where he'd gone?

Jesus, what time is it? Zoe never wore a watch so she pulled out her cell phone. Just then the sound of a turboprop coming in to land broke the silence. Had to be Aden's plane. Shit! About to leave, she remembered the calendar in the kitchen where they had always written appointments. Sure enough there it was, a pale rectangle on the side of the cupboards, but there was too little light left to read any of the notes on it. She pulled out her cigarette lighter. The last note, eight days ago, said 'AC7802> 6:05 a.m.', the early flight to Toronto. So he had been gone more than a week.

Hurriedly she left, replaced the key where she had found it and slogged back through the snow to her car. Aden was going to be pissed but that was almost a permanent condition these days.

By the time she got to the airport the airporter shuttle and some of the cars there to pick up passengers were already leaving. Pulling into a parking slot with twelve minutes left on the meter she was about to hurry in to face Aden's wrath when she stopped herself. Already feeling guilty about Connor, she couldn't face Aden right now. Getting back into her car, she started the engine for the warmth, cracked the window and lit a cigarette. The smell of cigarette smoke would be yet another indictment from her partner. So why do I put up with it, she wondered. We don't even like each other any more. And she thought about the remains of the day: all the way back into town, Aden would tell her what a useless piece of shit she was; how she couldn't even be on time for a plane that was an hour and a half late. As soon as they got home, Aden would be into the vodka; the silences would follow and finally Aden would either pass out or begin a new rant. Welcome to my world.

How had she reached this point? Connor had been off on a six-week photo shoot to Patagonia when Zoe had attended an opening at the Northern Enlightenment Art Gallery on

Elgin Street. The featured artist, Aden Bourassa, had recently gained a degree of notoriety when her work, *The Shroud of Mary Magdalene*, had been exhibited in Toronto. Barbara Hall, the Toronto Human Rights Commissioner, had denounced it as "both blasphemous and banal," and Reverend Thomas Collins, Archbishop of the Toronto diocese, had thundered that it was "an insult to the church and to women everywhere." Such comments proved to be pure gold to the media and Aden had achieved some fame as a result. Not surprisingly, the small gallery was full and many of the local glitterati stood outside in the warm evening air gulping wine and devouring cheese and crackers. Towards midnight the wine ran out and so did most of the crowd. Knots of people made their way to Peddler's Pub, Respect is Burning or the Laughing Buddha to continue the evening's festivities.

Finally Zoe had managed to get a close look at the shroud. The artist had painstakingly reproduced the shroud of Turin on a piece of what appeared to be linen of the same size as the original and in the same sepia tone with a couple of remarkable differences: the image in Aden's version was a female and, if the viewer looked closely enough, she could see that it was entirely made up of tiny dots. *The Shroud of Mary Magdalene* was laid out horizontally on a light table. The effect was eerie. On the wall behind the exhibit several smaller light boxes showed magnified sections of the piece revealing that each dot held a different image of Madonna, not the blessed virgin of legend, but the modern gap-toothed singer.

Zoe thought it a powerful work and was leaning over it when a voice behind her said, "Wondering why I didn't put the whole thing on the wall?"

Zoe turned to see Aden holding a tumbler that almost certainly contained something stronger than wine. "No. It seems exactly right as it is," she said.

"So many women earn their living on their backs, both literally and figuratively," said Aden, the excessive sibilance revealing that she was well past her first drink.

"You make it sound as if the symbolism is pretty heavy-handed," said Zoe. Aden scowled at her and for a moment Zoe thought she might get a drink in the face but she persisted. "What I mean is, the work doesn't need any explanation. It is what it is."

Aden hesitated for a moment between anger and acknowledgement before choosing the latter and holding out her hand. "Aden Bourassa."

"Zoe. I don't use a last name." They shook hands.

"My niece goes to your dance academy. She worships you."

They talked until, sometime after one, the gallery owner gently urged them out the door so she could close up. Aden had put her arm through Zoe's as they stood on the sidewalk. "My place isn't far from here," she told Zoe. "You know you really shouldn't be driving."

That night Zoe had had her first experience of love with another woman since she had attended the National Ballet School in her teens. For the next four weeks while Connor was away, she spent almost all her time with Aden. By the time Connor was due to return, the small arts community of Sudbury regarded them as a couple.

"What are you going to tell him?" Aden had asked the night before Connor's return.

"That I am in love with you, what else?"

"He'll be furious. If you think he might get violent, I could come with you. I always carry a knife."

"Good God, no. Connor's not like that."

"Most men are."

"Oh, bullshit."

Aden shrugged. "Have it your own way." For the next couple of hours, Aden retired to the attic where she worked.

The signs were there, Zoe told herself now, I just couldn't see them. We were both on our best behaviour in those first few months as most lovers are. And, of course, there was more than a touch of celebrity worship on my part. Only after she had made the commitment and moved in with Aden did she realize what she had got herself into. True, the last year had been a frustrating time for Aden. After the huge success of *The Shroud*, Aden felt the pressure to follow it up with something at least as impressive. Nothing seemed to be working. Depressed, she started drinking more than usual and, as often happens, taking out her frustrations on Zoe. At first Zoe just listened to the drunken rants, and put up with the silences that might last for days. More and more she thought of Connor, of the good times together, of his gentle nature. One day, she and Aden were watching the news when Connor came on the screen. "Not that asshole!" said Aden and reached for the remote.

"Leave it!" Zoe was surprised at the tone of command in her voice.

Aden stopped, hand outstretched. "What?"

"I said leave it."

Aden rose. At the door she turned and shouted, "How can you stand the sight of that talentless asshole?" then left without waiting for a reply.

Zoe was shaking from the confrontation but, at the same time, she felt triumphant as she watched Connor being interviewed about the award he had just received for his shoot in

Patagonia. For the next few days she wanted to call him. Just to congratulate him? No, she admitted to herself, she wanted to hear his voice again, maybe set up a meeting somewhere. She actually did call once but no one answered and she did not leave a message.

And now he had disappeared without even calling her. She took a deep breath, put the car into reverse and turned towards the exit. As she passed the main doors of the airport, Aden, stony-faced, emerged towing her luggage. For a fleeting second their eyes met. Aden's mouth opened and began to scream silent outrage into the cold air as Zoe turned her eyes back to the road. She was shaking as she pulled back on to Skead Road and headed towards town.

Five minutes later as she passed Connor's darkened house, she pulled out her cell phone and, despite the recent law forbidding it, hit the speed dial. "Brenda, any idea where Connor is?" she asked the voice at the other end.

All the way back to Aden's place, she listened to Brenda. Brenda told Zoe that she, too, was worried about Connor. Eventually Zoe learned that Connor had sold Brenda his business and told her he was heading for Cuba.

"Did he say why?"

"He said he thought he would make a documentary but he never picked up any of his video equipment." And then the kicker. "About the time he left, I ran into my friend, Denise. She works at the hospital. When I told her about buying the business from Connor, she said"—a sudden catch in her voice—"she said, 'That makes sense, I guess. I doubt he's got all that long.'"

Room 335 looks the same as it had two years ago when Connor had shared it with Zoe. The maid must still be the tiny Mariel. No one else graces the turned down bed with two kissing swans fashioned out of towels quite the way she does. Depositing his suitcase and carry-on next to the closet that holds the safe, Connor walks over to the window and looks out through the louvered shutters at the street below. For the first time since leaving Sudbury, he smiles. Good to be back in Havana. Suddenly he remembers standing in this very spot, his arms around Zoe, the two of them listening to a tenor running scales in the night.

"They're performing Tosca at the theatre just across the square," she had told him. "There's a poster in the lobby."

"Then we should go." And they had gone to see a touring Korean company performing in the ornate Gran Teatro across the square. Last show they had seen together.

With a sigh, he turns away, grabs his toilet kit out of the suitcase and goes into the familiar white-tiled bathroom. As he washes off the travel grime at the sink, Connor glances across at the shower and notes with satisfaction that the bracket for the shower head is still broken. Some things never seem to change. Feels good that time here seems to have stopped while his life has been disintegrating around him.

After washing down the pills Dr. Mallay had prescribed, he winks at himself in the mirror. "Wouldn't kick me out of Bulgaria now," he mutters, staring at the light bouncing off his shaved head. Years before, Connor had been denied entrance to Bulgaria because of his long hair. "Look a bit pale but a tan will fix that." And today he really does feel good. Maybe because finally he is on the move again.

The doorman nods as he opens the door of the Hotel

Plaza for Connor to step out. After flying into Havana from a Canadian winter, Connor welcomes the heat of the afternoon, the sight of palm trees. For a moment he stands there taking in Havana's Parque central with its famous old cars, angle-parked as always, and looming in the background above the trees, the dome of the Capitólio. A couple of taxi drivers parked in front of the Hotel Plaza offer their services but he politely declines. Instead he strolls down the yellow stone colonnade beside the hotel, across a cobblestone square, and through a line of cannons, their muzzles buried so that now they act as traffic barriers. There he waits for a bicitaxi to pass before crossing the Avenue de las misiones to the salmon-pink building on the corner.

The Floridita, the most famous bar in Havana, had once been a favourite of Earnest Hemingway. Behind the tiny bandstand, a bronze statue of him now leans on the end of the curved bar. The Floridita trades on Hemingway's famous quotation: "My mojito in La Bodeguita. My daiquiri in El Floridita." From its opening at eleven until late evening, day-tripping tourists from the buses out of the resorts along the coast crowd in, have their pictures taken with Hemingway's statue, and leave. When he was younger, Connor would have avoided places like this. Tourist traps he had called them. In those days, too, he would have insisted he was a traveller, definitely not a tourist. Age mellows us all, he guesses, because now despite the crowds and the high drink prices, Connor loves the place with its faded wallpaper, pictures of Hemingway around the walls, the friendly, efficient waiters and its claim to be "*la cuna del daiquiri*," cradle of the daiquiri.

He orders one now and checks his watch: 2:15 p.m. When he had called her just before he had caught the plane down to Toronto, he had told Lunaria he would meet her here at three. The band returns from a break and begins to play "*El Chan Chan*." His daiquiri arrives, a pyramid of ice topped by a sprig of mint. He takes a sip. Yes, they do still make the best daiquiris in Havana. The band is fronted by two women singers. The taller girl, who also plays the flute, looks a little like Lunaria. Watching her, he begins to feel nervous. How long has it been since he dated anyone? He had been with Zoe for more than twelve years.

Zoe. Their divorce had just become final when Connor had started to get the strange chest pains that finally drove him to see Dr. Mallay. Jan Mallay had been treating him for his asthma for years and so when she had called him in about the results of the tests, he knew by the tightness in her voice that something was seriously wrong. When he had asked her how long he had, she had said there was no way of knowing, could be years. "Towards the end, you may need some live-in help," she had concluded, "but when that will be, no one can tell you." Stunned by the news, he had sat in his truck for the longest time, staring through the windshield at the snowy mantle covering Memorial Park. The doctor's message: "Because of the damage the asthma has done to your lungs over the years, the blockages around your heart are inoperable." The single word, "inoperable," kept cycling around in his head.

When he got back to his empty house, early winter darkness had already erased the remains of the day. He had tried to distract himself by playing a couple of games on-line but the darkness that had descended on his future kept drawing him back. Call Zoe? And let her know just how right she had been to trade him in for a new lover? What had made him even more bitter was the fact that Aden, her new love interest, was a woman. He felt that behind the sympathy of his friends lay secret smiles of contempt. He knew he was touchy about the subject but still couldn't stop himself from cutting people off if they made even a veiled reference to Zoe. He had even hung up on his friend, Phil, who had speculated that it sounded as if Connor was still carrying a torch for Zoe. After a while people had stopped calling.

Restless now, he got up and wandered through the empty house. "Got to get out of here. Travel." He would sell his photography business to Brenda, his assistant. She was already doing much of the video work. He would give her a good price and she could pay him out of the future profits. Before he could change his mind, he called her at home.

"Of course, I'd love to take over, but why now?"

"I need to spend some time travelling. There's a documentary I'd like to work on. And life's too short so…"

"A documentary? Really? You've never mentioned one. On what?"

"Life in Cuba," he improvised. "You know, how things are changing now that Fidel has retired."

The explanation seemed to satisfy her, although she was, not surprisingly, intrigued when he had asked her to keep the sale a secret even after he had gone. "Just want to concentrate on the work, you know," he had said when she asked why. And never shoot another damn wedding, he added to himself as he hung up.

Why Cuba? He had wanted to visit again since the day he had returned from spending a month there two years before. Not so far from Canada that he could not get back in a hurry if the need arose. And, if he was being honest with himself, the idea that he might one day need live-in help had triggered thoughts of the nurse he had met in a Havana clinic.

After rummaging through his desk, Connor had found the piece of paper where she had printed her name, address and phone number but could not bring himself to call her that night. Her name was Lunaria and, over the next couple of days, he found himself thinking, even fantasizing, about her a great deal even though their only meeting had lasted no more than twenty minutes.

He remembered almost every detail of that visit to the *Dispensario para tuberculosis* in Havana. The night before he had coughed until dawn, scarcely able to lie down for more than a few minutes. His congestion had finally broken up as the early morning sun began to filter into their room. Feeling better, he peered at Zoe and saw that she was awake. "Let's get some breakfast," he had suggested.

Taking the elevator up to the fifth floor, they found the dining room almost deserted at that early hour and managed to nab one of the prized tables on the outdoor patio overlooking old Havana. While they ate, Zoe said "Let's hire a taxi, one of the old ones and just tour around. You think you're up for that?"

Connor nodded. "Che Guevara had bad asthma too. Did you know that?"

"Yes, I did as a matter of fact. Hey, maybe you should wear the Che beret I bought you."

He had laughed but then quickly stopped as he felt a coughing spasm coming on. He took a couple of wheezy breaths. "Last time I wore it, I got my butt pinched on *Obispo*. Twice. Not even the same woman."

"See. Cuban women think you're sexy. With your beard, you do look a little like Che...if the light is just right..."

"...and I'm wearing the beret."

A tour group arrives, files past the band and begins to flash pictures of each other with the bronze larger-than-life Ernest. Connor wonders just how many millions of pictures there are around the world of people sitting next to the bronze image of a writer few of them have ever read. How many knew that the figure with the beguiling smile had blown himself away with a shotgun? At least Hemingway had lived into his sixties. Connor looks around and notices a picture of Che. The *guerrillero heróico* had not even made it to his fortieth birthday.

After breakfast, he and Zoe had crossed over to the centre of the square. A couple of minutes later, standing across the street from the Hotel Inglaterra, Connor had flagged down a cherry-red 1954 Chevy Belaire convertible with cream-leather upholstery, and offered the driver thirty convertible pesos for the next couple of hours. Vincent, their driver, had taken them along the waterfront where they had seen Che's modest house, the old city walls, el Moro fortress and, in the distance, the smoking flare from the oil refinery. Hearing Connor cough, Vincent had explained that there was much respiratory illness downwind of the plant. Maybe it had been the sight of the smoking flame that had triggered Connor's attack. After a long coughing spasm, he used his inhaler. Not

wanting to disappoint Zoe, he told her he was feeling better
and they had entered the Catedral de San Cristóbal. Vincent
guided them down the side aisle to the small chapel beside the
altar. Having trouble getting his breath, Connor had started
to feel faint. For a minute or two, he had tried to fight it as
Vincent recounted his experiences while fighting in Angola,
his bitterness at the betrayals by the Russians. Eventually the
light-headedness got the better of Connor and he told Vincent
that he had to sit down. Concerned, Vincent and Zoe had led
him to a pew to rest. When Connor was feeling a little better,
Vincent had driven them to the clinic.

The waiting room had been a few garden benches arranged
around a small fountain in an airy courtyard. Within a couple
of minutes, he was conducted into one of the consulting
rooms. Soothing pastel green walls. The doctor had listened to
his chest and given him oxygen to breath through a glass tube
containing saline solution. He was impressed that she had not
even asked his name. The doctor had been kind but spoke
almost no English. The nurse, however, had caught his eye
and not just because she was fluent in English. Even without
the tight white uniform, Lunaria was a woman that would be
noticed anywhere.

"Where you from?" she had asked at once. When told
Canada, she had flashed a smile that lit up the room and
urged Zoe to take her picture. "In case any Canadians with
lots of money are looking for a Cuban *chica*." Zoe had laughed
and taken her picture after which Lunaria had written out
her name, address and telephone number and handed it to
her. "Maybe an old one," Lunaria had added with a laugh, "to
leave me lots of dollars." That was the picture they had sent to
Lunaria but there had been another one. The second picture

caught her kissing Connor lightly on the temple, her mischie-
vous brown eyes focused on Zoe's camera. That was the picture Connor liked best.

Thoughts of Lunaria led to memories of his three weeks
in Cuba with Zoe. "We're probably the last Canadians to visit
Cuba," Zoe had said as they sat on the veranda at the Colonial
in Baracoa drinking mojitos. "Why did we wait so long?"

"Because everybody else had already been here?"

"Except the Americans," she pointed out.

"And now we're here because of Obama."

"Right. Had to see it before he let the Americans in and
there's a KFC on every corner."

"And they buy up all the beachfront and the old cars."

"There goes the neighbourhood."

They had grown to love Cuba and the people, nowhere
more than Baracoa, the town isolated at the far eastern end of
the island.

After the bad news, Connor had begun to spend many
hours on the internet looking up Cuba websites. Gradually
his vague plan of just abandoning everything and going
back to Cuba, seeing Lunaria, spending whatever time he
had left with her, was beginning to seem much more than
just a possibility. Maybe he would even end up marrying
her. Marrying a Cubana seemed to be the only way to get
permanent residency in Cuba. Although most visas were for
thirty days, as a native-born Canadian, Connor could stay up
to six months. No guarantee he could extend his visa when it
ran out at the end of September though. He even toyed with
the idea that he would leave his worldly goods, few though
they were, to Lunaria. Why not? Zoe didn't need him so why
let her get his money. And half would go to Aden. "Whoa," he

cautioned himself. "Maybe you should let Lunaria in on this master plan."

Not until a couple of evenings later with the aid of a jug of homemade daiquiris had he pulled out the piece of paper with her number, reached for the phone...and hesitated. What time was it there? Ah, same as here, he remembered. Sudbury and Havana were within half a degree of longitude. "Nothing to lose, so no more excuses," he muttered to himself and punched in the number.

"I'm the Canadian you treated in the clinic almost two years ago," he had told her. Hardly better than "What's your sign?" he admitted to himself.

"Two years ago..." He could hear the hesitation in her voice, the Cuban accent even more pronounced on the phone.

"I sent a photograph to the address you gave us, one of you and me in the clinic." He had the picture of the two of them on the table in front of him.

She laughed. "Ah, I remember you, of course. You have found someone who is looking for a nice Cuban girl?"

"Well, yes. Me. I'm on my way to Havana and I was wondering if we could, you know, link up."

"But you are married, no? Your wife, she takes the picture."

"Zoe and I aren't married anymore. I'm single. So I thought..."

"Not married?" The tone was friendlier but still guarded.

"Not any more."

A few seconds of silence. "So you are looking for a wife, or just a good time with a Cuban *chica*?" Direct.

"That's what I want to talk to you about, Lunaria. I've been thinking about you a lot."

They had talked for an hour that time and several times since. He had told her about his illness, left out the grim diagnosis reasoning that she was a nurse and would put two and two together. Easier than telling her directly; easier, he had convinced himself, for both of them.

Eventually she agreed to take her vacation so that they could get to know each other. He suggested they meet in Havana and then spend the rest of her vacation in Baracoa.

"Not possible," she had told him. "The *policia* there check every hotel and the *casas particulares*. If they find me staying with a Canadian tourist, they could arrest me."

The next morning over coffee, he recalled his doctor telling him that eventually he might need some live-in help. Perfect. He called Lunaria with his brilliant idea. She had listened intently and laughed at its boldness. "Yes, it would work, but you would have to pay for two rooms and my salary."

"I would have done that anyway until you…until we… decided that we really, you know, were in love with each other."

She laughed again. "Are all Canadians so crazy as you?"

"You gotta be crazy to live in this climate."

He could hear her taking a deep breath. "All right. I'll need something from your doctor and you'll have to hire me as your nurse. This is *loco*, but…I've heard Baracoa is a very nice place. Book your flight and I'll arrange the time."

Lunaria's picture is in his wallet. Maybe I'll show it to her as an icebreaker when she arrives.

The musicians finish their set and Connor throws a three peso note into the hat when the taller girl approaches him. Then he checks his watch. Almost three. "Another one, *signor*?" asks the waiter as he whisks away Connor's empty glass.

"What? Oh, yes. *Si, si, gratias.*"

The bus tours have departed and the Floridita has sailed into the afternoon doldrums with no more than fifteen or so patrons scattered around. At the bar, a beautiful blonde with an English accent is smoking a cigarette and stroking an old guy with long grey hair. The guy looks vaguely familiar.

Connor has a need to piss that he can no longer ignore. What if she comes while he's in the Men's? He rises and crosses to the top of the bar, signals the waiter and tells him, "I'm expecting a friend. If she comes in while I'm in the toilet, you mind telling her to wait?"

The waiter nods.

An unusually pleasant washroom: pucks in the urinals and, even more unusual in Cuban bars, seats on the toilets. When he has washed his hands, he checks himself in the mirror before telling himself, "Not bad, but maybe you should have worn the beret."

Back in the bar, Connor looks over at the waiter who shakes his head. Better slow down on these, Connor tells himself when the next drink arrives. Don't forget they don't stint on the liquor in the drinks here. 3:10 p.m. No need to panic. Hey, she's Cuban after all. Caribbean time.

To distract himself, he lifts his shoulder bag from the chair beside him and pulls out the printout for the flight to Baracoa at the other end of the island. The plane leaves at 1:20 p.m. the next afternoon. Or thereabouts, he tells himself.

Fifteen minutes later the band is back. The taller woman smiles directly at him as they launch into "Bésame Mucho." He feels his stomach beginning to tighten. Caribbean time, he reassures himself. She lives in Vedado, that's the other side of town. God, this dating thing could have you sweating blood.

He looks over at the bar. The old guy with the blonde is gone. At least somebody scored this afternoon. Pulling out his wallet, he looks at Lunaria's picture. Drop dead gorgeous. He figures he's maybe fifteen years or so older than she is. So what? She was looking for somebody even older.

The band takes another break. And suddenly there she is, breezing through the door as if she owns the place. Connor rises to his feet and gestures to her to join him. She smiles, leaves her suitcase for the doorman to look after and rushes over to him, her heels clicking on the tiled floor.

She gives him a brief hug and kisses his cheek so that he can smell her perfume and then launches into an apology as she sits down. Connor just smiles at her and waits to get a word in. She came, she really came.

"…so my brother-in-law finally turned up with his car but first we had to take my aunt to the hair salon and…so here I am. Sorry I am late." She shrugs. "Cuba time, I guess."

The waiter appears and she orders a mojito but when Connor switches to *café con leche*, she orders one too. "Milk is rationed here," she explains, "so having milk in our coffee is a treat."

"Everybody seems well fed though."

"Oh, yes. It's just that sometimes the lack of things like soap or milk can get you down."

As Lunaria talks on about life in Cuba, Connor realizes that she has been as nervous as he but now they seem to be starting to relax.

"You look well," she tells him as she finishes her coffee; "much better than when I saw you last."

"Actually, I've been feeling pretty good, last few days. And seeing you again…well, how do you say it in Spanish, '*muy buena*'"?

"*Si. Gratias*, Connor."

Lunaria talks about all the arrangements she has made and how much she is looking forward to going to Baracoa. "Did you book rooms there?"

"Sure did."

"At a *casa*?"

"No. I didn't think you'd want to stay with a family so I booked us in to the Hotel La Rusa. It's a little hotel right on the Malecón so most of the rooms have a view of the sea. I spent a pleasant afternoon there once a couple of years ago. You know, Che stayed there once. They've even got a sign outside his room. And Errol Flynn."

"Errol Flynn?"

"An actor. Before your time. Hell, before my time."

Lunaria put her arm through his. "You know this still seems like some kind of a dream. But don't wake me up."

"May all your dreams come true then." He checks his watch. Almost five. Where has the time gone? "Look. Let's get you checked in. You're room is next to mine at the Plaza. Number 333."

While Connor is paying the tab, the band filters back in. Behind him, he hears a shriek and looks around as the waiter gives him his change. The tall woman who had been playing the flute with the band is hugging Lunaria. The two are talking rapidly in Spanish. When he approaches, Lunaria introduces him to her cousin. "I told her you are my patient," she prompts.

"And I couldn't have found a better nurse," he says to the cousin.

"Oh, Lunaria will look after you very well," she tells him. Both women laugh. "And in Baracoa. I hear it is wonderful this time of year."

"Yes, I was there a couple of years ago. Great place."

"I would miss Havana though. Have a great time. *Chao.*"

"*Chao,*" Connor says.

Checking Lunaria in seems to take forever. Connor's smattering of Spanish is no match for the rapid conversation between Lunaria and the woman behind the desk but he notices the clerk's attitude shift from suspicion to acceptance as Lunaria produces yet another document from her voluminous purse. Finally, the woman hands Lunaria the electronic key card to her room, smiles at them and says in English, "Enjoy your stay with us."

When they get to her room, Lunaria puts the card in the slot and tries the handle but nothing happens. Gently, Connor takes the card from her, shows her the arrow and says, "You just put it in the slot with the arrow pointing down and pull it out. See? The green light goes on."

"Thanks, Connor," she says.

"I love the way you pronounce my name," he says as he pushes back the door.

"I don't say it right?"

"No, no. It sounds better. Rhymes with *Señor.*"

"You like it like that? Con-nor?"

"*Si*, 'Con-nor' sounds great."

Lunaria nods and looks around the room. She smiles broadly and points at the towel swans. "Beautiful. You know, Connor, I have lived in Havana all my life but this is the first time I have seen inside this hotel. "Is beautiful." She wanders into the bathroom. Not wanting to crowd her, Connor waits between the door and the bar fridge in the corner. "My God! Soap," he hears from the bathroom. She comes to the door and shows him the two small bars still in their ornate wrapping.

"We leave tomorrow, yes?"

"Yes."

She nods and pops one of the bars into her purse. "Is hard to get here."

Connor puts his hand on the door handle and checks his watch. "I'll let you unpack then," he says, feeling suddenly shy. As he begins to open the door, she crosses and stops him.

Reaching up, she kisses him on the lips, surprising him. So long since anyone at all has touched him. An unaccustomed feeling that he takes a moment to identify as gratitude. Connor throws his arms around her but she pushes him gently away and says, "Later. Give me time to change and let's go for a meal."

"Sure," he says, slightly ashamed at his own eagerness.

Lunaria gently kisses him again and whispers, "Give me an hour."

Connor lies propped up on the bed flipping channels on the small television, surprised that two of the channels appear to be Chinese. Finally he finds CNN in English. The commercials have been stripped from the feed and the resulting repetition of stories lulls him to sleep. He wakes in a panic to find that it is almost eight o'clock. He was supposed to be at her door an hour ago. Hurriedly he shoves his passport and the extra wallet bulging with convertible pesos into the safe and locks it. Then after a last look around, he hurries next door.

When she opens the door, he launches into an apology before she puts her finger on his lips and says, "Don't worry. There was lots on TV. I almost forgot the time myself."

Later, as they pass the Floridita and turn up Obispo, a cobblestoned pedestrian thoroughfare lined with restaurants, she puts her arm through his. Connor guesses that she has waited until they are out of sight of the hotel. "Where are we going?" she asks.

"A restaurant I know off the square at the end of Obispo. It's called Al Medina."

"Al Medina?"

"It's an Arab restaurant. I discovered it last time I was here." Zoe had loved Al Medina so much they had eaten there three times. They stroll up the street, past the Florida and Ambos Mundos Hotels, through a deserted construction zone. "What are they doing?" Connor asks as they skirt a pile of cannons that appear to have been dug out of the road.

Lunaria laughs. "They are digging up the asphalt and putting down cobblestones. Only in Cuba would they do this."

"Why?"

"Part of the restoration. Havana is a world heritage site."

Lunaria is suitably impressed by the pleasant courtyard illuminated by strings of lights in the trees. He orders the lamb tagine and Lunaria the cous cous with a side order of pita bread and hummus. Connor has spent so much time alone recently that he is content to let Lunaria lead the conversation at first. Gradually, with the help of a bottle of wine and the encouragement of his bubbly companion, he becomes more confident and begins to talk about himself, leaving out all but the briefest mentions of Zoe but talking at length about his interest in photography, about Canadian winters and about his impressions of Baracoa. Lunaria's narrative is also incomplete as she tells him about growing up in Cuba before the Russians left and about her job. Just as Connor has not mentioned Zoe, Lunaria omits Alexei from her biography. Charming but lazy, Alexei, her Russian husband, had returned to Russia three years before. The divorce had finally come through a few months ago. And now this Canadian had booked them into at a hotel called La Rusa. Would that bring her more bad luck?

Connor had stopped talking and was looking at her quizzically. I must look as if I am not interested, Lunaria chided herself. "What is cibachrome?" she asks, fastening on his last phrase. "I don't know the word."

"Yeah, of course. Most Canadians don't know what it is either." Securely within his own area of expertise, he tells her that although almost all his work is digital now, he still prefers the vibrant images yielded by the old analog process. Lunaria understands little of what he is telling her but is happy to listen, to watch the sparkle in his eyes as he tells her of the international awards his prints have won, of growing his business, of his disappointment that most of his work was for weddings and civic functions. "Not only are the Cibachrome colours brilliant but they never fade, even in sunlight. Funny though, the only picture I brought with me was taken by someone else with a point-and-shoot." When he pulls out his wallet to pay the bill, he shows Lunaria the picture of her kissing him on the temple.

"My God, I was really in a crazy mood that day." They laugh.

On the way back, they stop at the Castillo de farnes, a popular bar not far from their hotel. They manage to get a table outside under the awning where they can watch the hookers plying their trade. Across the street three bored policemen lounge in an old Lada with a blue light on top.

When the drinks come, she toasts, "To us."

"To us."

"Now we will be lucky," Lunaria tells him. "In this same bar Che and Fidel toasted the success of the revolution."

Before they are finished their drinks, the bar starts to

empty. Connor checks his watch: getting on for midnight when almost all entertainment in Cuba stops. The bar at the Plaza must have a special dispensation because it stays open twenty-four hours.

As they reach Lunaria's room, Connor feels himself getting nervous again, unsure how to proceed. At her door, Lunaria takes charge, thanking him for a wonderful evening and kissing him passionately before putting her key card in the slot and pulling it out.

"You see, I learned something new today." She kisses him again and asks, "What time is breakfast?"

"Around nine? We don't have to be at the airport before noon and there's always a taxi outside."

"Nine is fine. Until then." A smile and then she is gone.

Barely an hour later, Connor is cursing his own sentimentality. Why had he decided on the same room that he had shared with Zoe? The congestion in his chest has flared up again and, despite his various medications, he has to stack the pillows against the backboard and try to doze in front of the tiny television. Perhaps something in the room is triggering his reaction, one of the legion of allergens that can make his life miserable. Still, he is excited by the prospect of taking Lunaria to Baracoa. At least they are staying at Hotel La Rusa, not at the *casa particular* on calle Frank País where he had stayed with Zoe. That decision had been easy. He certainly had not wanted Jacqui, the woman who ran the *casa*, wondering why he was returning without Zoe…and accompanied by a *cubana*. Thinking of Lunaria's kiss, he drifts off to sleep around four and does not wake until nearly nine.

As they take the short bus ride across the tarmac, Connor looks around and is not surprised to find that he is the only non-Cuban among the thirty or so passengers on Aero Caribbean Flight 440. Some are carrying cardboard boxes wrapped with tape. Lunaria suddenly grabs Connor's hand as the bus stops behind a stubby jet and says nervously, "This is my first time in an aeroplane."

Connor looks down into her luminous brown eyes and says, "You'll be fine. Don't forget, it's safer than driving."

"I was in a car accident once."

"See. Cars are more dangerous." Or maybe not, he thinks as he looks up at the battered old Russian Yak 40. But the flight is smooth and Lunaria's nervousness disappears when she plane reaches cruising altitude.

They touch down in less than two hours on the single airstrip at Gustavo Rizo airport. "Baracoa," Connor announces as they step out of the terminal. Lunaria laughs and says something to an old man sitting on a low wall on the island in the middle of the circular driveway. He nods and gestures towards her. She runs across in front of a bicitaxi and hands him her little camera. How do Cuban women put that hip action into their step, Connor wonders as he watches her.

"We need a picture," she tells the startled Connor as she runs back across the road in her high heels. The old man snaps the shot. Lunaria hands him a couple of peso notes as he returns the camera. He looks puzzled.

"He wasn't too pleased," Lunaria explains. "I gave him nationales, you know real pesos, not convertibles. They are worth much, much less." Impulsively she hugs him.

Connor smiles and silently congratulates himself on bringing her to Baracoa. "Let's get a taxi, Lunaria."

Lunaria nods, "That one over there." She is pointing to a taxi parked at the little refreshment stand to their right.

"The driver's eating, probably off duty," Connor tells her.

"Don't worry," she says and puts two fingers in her mouth to produce an ear-splitting whistle.

"Holy shit!" says Connor. The cabbie, along with almost everyone else who is milling around, looks in their direction. Lunaria yells at him and he responds with a world-weary shrug. "Come on."

The cab driver mops up the last of his black beans and rice, wipes his hands and starts to load their luggage into the trunk. Just then the roar of a propeller aircraft makes them turn. An old Antonov 2 passenger biplane is dropping out of the blue sky over the town. Connor's Nikon is in his hand in an instant and he is running, actually running, to the slight rise on the island in the middle of the circular driveway. There he stops, steadies himself and begins shooting.

"He is a big time photographer. Wins many awards," Lunaria tells the taxi driver. The cabbie nods wearily and climbs into the driver's seat. He has seen the old Russian Antonov 2 many times as it flies in the mail and newspapers almost every day.

"Did you see that?" Connor asks as he returns.

"Yes. I am glad that was not our plane." She notes with relief that, despite the run, his breathing is only slightly faster than usual.

"It's amazing. I saw it once when I was here before. It flew right over us when we were sitting in a bar just off the Plaza Independencia. Amazing they still fly them."

"Old planes, old cars, even old steam engines. We Cubans try to keep everything going forever."

"And it's great."

She thinks of telling him that it is not always great to have to reuse and repair things all the time but he is so eager, so, well, Canadian. Instead she says, "Everyone who comes here seems to like our old things."

"Yeah. We do. This cab looks brand new though."

Lunaria nods as Connor opens the back door of the cab and helps her in. "It's a Geely," she says, as he settles in beside her. "Most of our new cars seem to come from China these days."

"Hotel La Rusa," he tells the driver.

As they drive around Baracoa Bay into the town, Connor notes with pleasure that most of the traffic is still powered by human or horse power. One of the reason he finds the place so charming is the clean air. The driver looks in his mirror, catches Lunaria's eye and says something in Spanish. She translates: "He says he can't take the Malecón, you know, the coast road, because the sea is coming over the sea wall."

"At our hotel, we'll have a front row seat," Connor tells her, excited by the prospect. Waves crashing over the seawall and across the road next to the yellow Hotel La Rusa is the most vivid image that comes to mind whenever he recalls his time in Baracoa. It was the image of the wild surf that helped persuade him to book La Rusa. He had rejected the better known Hotel El Castillo on top of the hill. Blessed with beautiful views of Baracoa, the sea, and the mountains behind the town, El Castillo also stands at the top of a daunting flight of steps .

The driver turns down calle Antonio Maceo. "Look how high the sidewalks are on this side," he points out. "My guess is that even here, three or four blocks up from the sea, they get flooding in hurricane season."

Lunaria is uncharacteristically quiet but because of Connor's enthusiasm, and the fact that he and Lunaria had really only met yesterday, he fails to notice. Such a small, backward place,

Lunaria thinks as they drive past a crowd of idle bicitaxis and their riders. Already she is missing the bustle of Havana.

"This is the Plaza Independencia," Connor tells her as the taxi slows to turn left towards the sea just before reaching the wedged shaped park with the ruins of the Catedral de la Asunción looming up behind it. "It has some good clubs, art galleries. You'll love it."

Lunaria smiles and squeezes his arm. "Yes, I love it already."

As they approach the Hotel La Rusa, they hear the crashing surf before it comes into view. And suddenly, although the sky is clear and blue, a three meter wave rears up and splinters into white spray that floods across the Malecón no more than a hundred metres from La Rusa.

"Wow! See that?"

"Why is it so rough?" Lunaria asks, clinging tightly to his arm. "The sky is clear."

Connor realizes, all at once, that Lunaria has lived through several hurricanes. "Probably a storm miles out to sea," he says. "It'll calm down soon."

Connor has booked adjoining rooms as before and while he is busy checking in, Lunaria walks over to the wall to the left of the desk and looks at four framed pencil sketches of the same beautiful young woman. "La Rusa?" she asks the woman behind the desk.

"Yes. They were sketched in 2005 from actual pictures taken when she was in her twenties."

"She's beautiful," Connor observes. "I'm guessing from the hairdo she was a flapper."

"She was a princess, *señor*," the woman replies. "Her name was Magdalena Ruvenskaya but her friends called her Mina. When she was a child, her family had to flee the Russian Revolution. She roamed the world working as a dancer and a singer until she came to Baracoa in the fifties and opened this hotel."

"She has passed away of course," Lunaria says.

"Many years ago. May I have your *carnet?*" the woman asks Lunaria who hands over her identity card.

"Some patrons say they have seen her on the landing at night," the woman tells them while she writes down Lunaria's particulars. Like most businesses in Cuba, the hotel lacks a computer.

When the woman hands Lunaria's papers back, Connor is surprised by a quick exchange in Spanish. Connor is wondering what the woman said but just then she passes them the keys to rooms 304 and 305 and, dismissing them with a cheerful *"Bienvenidos a La Rusa,"* hurries into the Magdalena Bar to serve a patron.

The marble stairs are narrow and steep and set at eccentric heights so Connor is puffing by the time they reach the next floor. To disguise his need to rest, he leans on the railing and asks Lunaria, "What was the woman telling you?"

Lunaria hesitates and then says, "I asked if she had ever seen the ghost. She told me only three or four people had seen it over the years and she blamed it on too many mojitos."

"And you don't?"

"I saw my father's ghost in my room the night he was killed in Angola in 1988. I was only seven."

"Sorry, I didn't mean…"

"It's all right. I still think of him though." She is beginning to trust me, he tells himself, pleased.

"One more flight," he tells her. This one is longer but the steps are more regular.

The rooms are smaller than they had looked in the picture

at the travel website but they are clean and comfortable. The bathroom has the same white tiles as the one in Havana and in almost every other bathroom in Cuba The bathroom is so small it holds a shower instead of a bath. At least the toilet has a seat.

Lunaria and Connor have become comfortable enough with each other to leave their doors open while they unpack. So it is that Connor can hear Lunaria's cry of delight as she looks out the window at the view of the sea, the Malecón and, beyond the outskirts of the town, the mountains. Any lingering doubts that Connor had had about his retreat to Baracoa drop away.

In his own room, Connor too has been staring out the window at the waves crashing over the seawall. Four little boys are running through the spray and laughing. He begins to laugh softly himself. Arms encircle him and he feels the warmth of Lunaria pressing against his back. Startled and delighted, he turns to find her smiling at him.

"I locked the door," she tells him.

He looks down into her brown eyes and says, "Man, I am the luckiest guy in the world."

She kisses him and then lets her robe drop to the floor. Her brown body is illuminated by a single shaft of sunlight from the window. "My God," he thinks, "it's been…" but she kisses his thoughts away while she expertly undoes his belt and helps his dockers slide to the floor. "We will make love gently," she whispers to him and turns away to pull back the yellow coverlet and stack the pillows. Then she leads him to the bed and has him lie down with his head and shoulders propped by the pillows. "Better for your lungs," she tells him. As she straddles him, he notices that her pubic mound is hairless, waxed smooth. A fleeting thought of Zoe's white v…and then no thoughts, only the present moment.

Afterwards, Lunaria insists on Connor taking his various medicines and tells him to rest for a couple of hours before they go out. He agrees. Still easily tired, he is sure he can already feel the clean salt air of Baracoa and the presence of Lunaria improving his health. While Connor sleeps, she sits on the other bed watching the tiny TV with only a whisper of sound.

Connor awakes to the sound of his name being gently whispered in his ear: "We should go out if we are going to get something to eat."

With a jerk he sits up and swings his legs over the edge of the bed. A deep breath and he smiles, feeling fine. The bedside light is on and darkness leans against the windows. "How long was I asleep?" he asks.

"Three, three and a half hours maybe."

He nods and says, "I'd better have a shower."

She kisses his forehead and heads for the door. "Call me when you're ready."

"About ten minutes then, and…" Lunaria hesitates at the door, "that was wonderful."

She laughs and says, "Me too. Now hurry up. I'm hungry."

As he emerges from the shower, he notices that the television is still on, an episode of *Friends*." *Amigos* in Cuba, he guesses.

When Lunaria opens the door at his knock, she is wearing high-heeled sandals, purple capri pants and a tight-fitting top with a glittering sunburst pattern.

"Wow! You look fabulous," Connor says.

"You like it?" She pirouettes to give him the full effect before posing with one hip out.

"I love it."

As they exit Connor's room, Lunaria points to a plaque on the wall next to room 302 across the hall. In Spanish, the legend says that Che Guevara stayed in this room, May 25th, 1961.

"This hotel is full of ghosts. Maybe one of us could move in there if we asked at the desk."

But Maritsa at the desk tells them that the room is occupied for the next week and, besides, it is very small. They thank her and head up through the darkened streets towards the Paladar Colonial, a privately owned restaurant.

At the Colonial they stop for a moment to watch the chess game going on at one end of the large veranda before finding a table in the dining room next to the small courtyard where a couple of ducks are wandering around eating bugs and sampling a small mound of rice.

Connor orders the pork dish which comes with *moros y cristianos*, the ever popular black beans and rice. Lunaria goes for the swordfish. When it comes, she feeds a forkful to Connor who pronounces it excellent. In reality, he finds it bland. One of the things he misses in Cuba is spicy food.

The next day they breakfast late and take a walk along the waterfront. The sea is calmer today. In the afternoon, Connor rests but not before promising Lunaria a spectacular sunset. He does not mention he intends to stop at the *casa particular* where he had stayed with Zoe. In a town this small, he knows he will eventually run into Jacqui, the woman whose house he and Zoe had shared for four days. Because he knows that Lunaria might feel awkward, he puts off telling her until they are turning up calle Frank País.

"Mind if we stop off at the *casa* I stayed in last time I was here?" Connor asks, as if the idea has just occurred to him.

"Sure, if you want to." Lunaria forces a smile.

"Better say hello. Beats running into her at the *mercado.*"

Ahead Connor can already see the corner house, one wall pink, one green. In front of the small raised veranda with its two wooden chairs is the ancient, twisted fire hydrant that he had joked about with Zoe as they sat outside writing postcards. "You'll like Jacqui," he tells Lunaria. "She's a great person. Really looked after us."

Connor steps on to the veranda and knocks at the open door. Jacqui appears and does not recognize him. She is a slim Afro-Cuban woman, her face dominated by her large dark eyes.

"I stayed here a couple of years ago," he tells her.

Her face lights up with sudden recognition. "Yes, of course. With your wife, ah…"

"Zoe. We're not married any more," Connor adds hurriedly. "I'm Connor, Jacqui. And this is my nurse, Lunaria."

"Ah, yes. You were not well when you arrived here from Santiago," Jacqui says. Jacqui has been trying to decide who Connor's companion is. Now she relaxes and invites them in.

As Jacqui ushers them through the living room Connor notes that the small television and stereo are still swathed in plastic when no one is using them.

They sit in the familiar dining room while Jacqui goes back to the kitchen to get them coffee. Connor points towards a curtain: "Our room was through there, even had its own bathroom…"—he lowers his voice—"but the air conditioner rattled like hell and there was no seat on the toilet. Jacqui was great though."

Lunaria is uncharacteristically silent, contemplating the ghost of Connor's former wife. Eventually she points to one of the objects on the shelves. "She has been to the Basilica de

Nuestra Señora del Cobre."

Connor looks over at the small glass cylinder with a statue of the virgin inside. "The church of the copper virgin," he says, proud of his increasing grasp of Spanish. "Yes. We stopped there too just outside Santiago. I still have a little chip of copper ore that a boy gave me at the door of the church."

Over the next few minutes, the silence stretches until Jacqui comes in with a tray and serves the coffee. Connor is beginning to realize that he should have come alone.

"Where are you staying?" Jacqui asks.

"We have two rooms at La Rusa," Lunaria volunteers. "Very comfortable."

"Ah." Jacqui turns to Connor. "What brings you back to Baracoa?"

"The clean air. I couldn't think of a better place to spend a few months. And to see you, of course. You were great to us last time."

Jacqui smiles and turns to Lunaria. "Did he tell you how good he is at doing the washing?"

Connor smiles. "No. Last time I was here, we ran out of clean clothes. Zoe asked Jacqui if she could use her washing machine. Jacqui pointed to the sinks. Zoe said there was no way she'd beat her washing on the sink and left in a huff. I borrowed some washing powder from Jacqui and scrubbed the clothes in the sink. After that I hung them up on the roof in the sun. I didn't think it was that big a deal but Jacqui thought the idea of a man doing the washing was hilarious."

"And then he bought me a large bag of washing soap. Not easy to get here."

"I know," says Connor. "The market had a guard on the door and there were only three bags of laundry soap left."

Jacqui and Connor laugh at the memory. Lunaria manages a smile.

"Another *café*?" asks Jacqui.

"Sure," says Connor, but when Lunaria declines, he realizes that he should have turned down the coffee too.

As he sips it, neither woman speaks. Both are looking at him. "You always did make great coffee," Connor says to break the silence but his comment is followed by another silence. Connor drinks the coffee so fast it scalds his mouth. "Guess we'd better get going," he says as he sets down his cup. Great to see you again, Jacqui."

As they leave, Jacqui urges them to drop by again but each one of them is sure that will never happen.

At the bottom of the steps up to the Hotel El Castillo, two young men stripped to the waist and sporting boxing gloves stop sparring and step aside for them. God, it looks like Everest, Connor thinks as they start up, but they rest at the first landing and when they finally make it to the top he is pleased to find that though he is a little short of breath he is not gasping for air. And the view. He puts his arm around Lunaria and says, "*Muy buena*. The view I mean."

"Is very beautiful." Below them, the red roofs of the town and beyond that the aching blue of the Atlantic Ocean and the Caribbean sky.

"See." Connor points to the yellow building far to their right, nestled beside the sea. "There's our hotel."

They walk through the Hotel El Castillo lobby and out to the patio. A few tourists are lounging around the pool.

"This is a beautiful hotel," says Lunaria, "and with a pool."

"And a spectacular view," Connor adds, "so why didn't I book us in here?"

"La Rusa is a nice hotel too," says Lunaria hurriedly.

"But it doesn't have a pool. I didn't book here because the reviews on the net were not all that good. The main reason, though, was those damn steps. I couldn't face that climb two or three times a day. Mind you there is a road that curves up here but it's too steep for bicitaxi drivers. Drink?"

"Tucola, or Coca Cola if they have it."

"At a tourist hotel, I'd bet on it. How else would you make Cuba libres?"

The sun is beginning to set as Connor brings her a coke and takes a sip of his mojito. "Seems the Coke is imported from Mexico. El Yunque," he says, gesturing at the flat-topped mountain now framed by a sky banded with multiple shades of scarlet laid on with broad strokes.

"I can see why they call it el Yunque. It looks like a…what is the English word?"

"Anvil."

She tries out the new word carefully.

"And over there," he points off to their right, "is the bay we drove around coming in from the airport. Beyond that you can see the airstrip."

Lunaria nods. "It doesn't look big enough to land on."

Connor laughs. "It almost isn't."

As the last of the light leaches out of the sky and a scattering of street lights come on in the town, they begin to descend the steps. On the way down, Connor tells Lunaria that for a couple of convertible pesos, she can come up and swim in the pool.

Because the exercise is good for Connor, climbing to El Castillo two or three times a week becomes part of their routine. Lunaria always brings a towel.

Wedged between the sea and the mountains, Baracoa

does not attract many tourists even in the high season. A few fly in from Havana and a half a dozen buses a week risk the winding Lighthouse Road, known locally as La Farola, but the road through the Sierra Maestra mountains from Santiago only gets more treacherous in May when the rains come and the heat begins to rise. Then Baracoa's four hotels lie almost empty and most of the *casas particulares*, each with a blue anchor, sign of government approval, shut up their rented rooms for the season.

During his first weeks back in Baracoa, Connor's Spanish has been improving under Lunaria's tutelage. While he is not yet fluent enough to carry on more than a halting conversation, he finds he is beginning to understand and piece together more of what is being said. And a curious thing happens. As the local people realize that the nurse and her patient are actually staying here they become more friendly, so that formal handshakes are replaced by a kiss on the cheek from the women, and a muscular handshake and half-embrace from the men.

Connor delights in the small exchanges that each day brings: trying out his Spanish with Ernesto when he goes to El Figaro, the tiny barber shop up the street, for a straight razor shave; talking baseball to the bartender at El Castillo while Lunaria swims in the pool; visiting the Casa de Chocolate to see if they actually have chocolate today; eating pizza from the street sellers; visiting the bookstore near Plaza Marti to find it has only four English books in its small collection. Lunaria asks Victor, the tall, stooped bookseller, if he has a copy of *La consagración de la primavera* by Alejo Carpentier, one of Cuba's most famous writers. Victor shrugs and admits he has not got a copy before pointing in his self-deprecating way at the multiple copies of a biography of Karl Marx. "That is what they send me," he tells her. But then he remembers that a friend has a copy and offers to see if he wants to sell it. Two days later, Victor arrives at the hotel with the book. He apologizes because the cover is on upside down. Connor laughs and gives him five convertibles.

In the evening Connor and Lunaria sometimes dine at La Rusa but more often they walk or take a bicitaxi to one of the *paladars*, private restaurants restricted to no more than twelve seats.

One leisurely evening after supper when they are relaxing in the rocking chairs on the large veranda of the Colonial, a small black dog with bright eyes, fox-like ears and a prettily feathered tail wanders up the steps and comes directly to Connor.

"My God, he is so cute," Lunaria says as the dog puts his front paws on the arm of Connor's chair. Connor laughs and pets him.

"I've seen him on the street. Always wandering around, looking busy. Hi, boy." The dog nuzzles his hand. "Sit." The dog does a complicated little dance and looks hopefully at Connor. "Oh, right, of course, he only understands Spanish. *Buenas noches, perro negro.*"

"See, now he is sitting," laughs Lunaria.

The dog follows them back to the hotel but shows no desire to go in. Over the next few days, whenever Connor takes a short walk along the seawall, the dog appears out of nowhere and walks beside him. Most mornings when he and Lunaria come down for breakfast in the covered patio bar, the little black dog is waiting for them, sitting on the low curved wall that graces a tiny traffic island no more than twenty metres from their table. Connor ignores him while he eats his breakfast: fruit, a ham omelet when there are eggs, toast and *café con leche*. Lunaria sticks to the ham and cheese sandwiches. Both of them save a little ham and toast for the dog.

On Connor's good days, when the two of them explore the town, the dog often tags along.

But there are days when Connor is too tired or too short of breath to do more than sit at one of the tables and watch the passing parade. At first, Lunaria stays with him and reads a book, but Connor can see that she is bored so he lets her know that he will be perfectly all right by himself. "Abelardo and Maritsa will look after me," he tells her, referring to the barman and the front desk clerk.

"I could help out at the Ciencias Medicas," Lunaria tells him.

"The clinic two doors down from the *Colonial*?"

"*Si*, the one with the painting of Che on the wall. It is close and if you needed me, I could be back in two minutes."

"Then it's settled." She reaches over and kisses him just as Maritsa appears.

"Anything else?" she asks, smiling at them both.

"Not right now," Connor tells her.

La Rusa's Magdalena bar is only accessible through the door to the lobby so there are never any *jitineros*, Cuban touts, in the bar itself. In an alcove off to the right, a couple of stools front the bar itself. The door beyond leads to the covered patio where Connor often sits at the second of the five tables, looking out at the Malecón framed by the low stone wall running the length of the patio and the rough trellis work that decorates the spaces between the posts supporting the overhanging roof.

Here he is content to spend hours reading, listening to

his music, and gazing out at the sweeping curve of the sea
wall and the Malecón until they disappear past the crumbling
baseball stadium. There the road leaves the sea and begins to
ascend towards the chocolate farms and jungle-clad hills, the
mountains and La Farola. To the east of the stadium, the curve
of the bay turns to jungle edged with black sand beaches and
ends in a spit of land that reaches a finger out into the Atlantic.

Except when the seas crash over the seawall and explode
across the road, the Malecón is a fairly busy place. Every
morning the truck loaded with school children in their red
and white uniforms goes by. Less welcome every day is the
banana man's appearance. Beyond the low patio wall he stops
and waves a bunch of bananas. After the first few days of this
Connor has had enough and barks, "*¡Andate a la mierda!*" but
the banana man just laughs and turns up the next day. Connor
smiles too at such dogged persistence.

More welcome are the visits of Frank, the bicitaxi driver
that he met one night at the Colonial. Frank had once been
a professional boxer and fought in Canada so his English is
passable. When they first met, Frank had showed his battle
scars, the wrist that rattled when he moved it, the crushed
nose cartilage and the heavy scar tissue over his eyes. They had
struck up an odd friendship so that sometimes Frank drops by
the hotel, picks Connor up and drives him around town in his
bicitaxi. Connor enjoys these impromptu outings. The need
to avoid the police, because carrying foreigners is illegal, adds
to the excitement on a dull afternoon. Often their rides end at
the Colonial for a couple of afternoon mojitos.

On afternoons when Frank fails to appear, Connor listens
for the rhythmic call of the peanut seller, "*Mani! Mani!...
Mani! Mani!*" When he appears at the other side of the low

wall, Connor greets him by name, gives him a convertible peso and takes four of his small cones of red, roasted peanuts. Then he orders a Bucanero beer and peels the paper wrapping off the best peanuts he has ever tasted. Usually, but not always, he manages to save one cone for Lunaria. As he shakes the last peanut out of each cone, he carefully unwraps the paper because Wiljum, the *mani* man, always wraps his peanuts in pages from an ancient Spanish encyclopaedia. Today page 4013 describes the operation of "*el submarino*" and, dictionary on hand, Connor puzzles through the Spanish.

Some days Connor reads *Granma*, the government newspaper that features articles by Fidel but little news of the world outside Cuba and Latin America. In Havana there is an English edition but only Spanish copies make it as far as Baracoa.

Often Connor will look up from the newspaper and see the black dog sitting on the wall of the tiny traffic island. Connor only has to nod and, with an effortless leap, the dog clears the low stone wall, curls up under Connor's table and is no trouble for the rest of the day.

When she is working at the clinic, Lunaria usually returns around four. Connor looks forward to her gossip about what is going on in town. When she changes and comes down to the bar, the dog always disappears almost as if his shift is finished. "I finally gave him a name," he tells Lunaria late one afternoon.

"Your little black dog?"

"*Mi perro negro? Si.*"

"Ah, good accent. So what are you calling him?

"You know that little dance he does?"

"Yes."

"Well, I called him 'Tango.'"

∾

By the second week of May the rains have begun to fall almost constantly. At breakfast on the sixth day of soft steady rain, Lunaria suggests that they walk up to *El Castillo* so he can get some exercise. "We'll take it easy up the steps."

"It's raining," Connor objects.

"Yes, but it is wonderful. How are you getting on with that book from Victor?"

"The one about Magdalena Rubenskaye? *La consagración de la primavera?*"

"*La Rusa*? *Sí*. You're beginning to sound like a real Cuban."

Connor shrugged, pleased by the compliment. "It's slow and some of the words are not in my dictionary."

"Because the dictionary is Spanish, not Cuban. Anyway Alejo Carpentier loved the rain in Baracoa. He called it the consecration of spring, devoid of all violence."

"Oh yes, I remember reading that part," he lies. Probably one of the passages he had skipped but he was not about to confess it.

"Would you like me to read it aloud to you sometimes when you are resting?" Lunaria asks him.

Connor nods. "Yeah, I'd like that a lot. Another *café con leche?*"

"So are we going up to El Castillo?" Lunaria asks again.

"Yes, yes, of course. I should get some exercise. Let's go."

Lunaria claps her hands in anticipation. "Wonderful! We'll even stop at the chocolate shop on the way back. I'll get changed." Smiling, she jumps up and heads upstairs.

Connor smiles to himself as he finishes his coffee. I doubt

I ever had as much energy as Lunaria, he tells himself. Making that phone call had been one of the best decisions he had ever made. A couple of times, he has even been tempted to whisper to her, "*Te amo*," but has stopped himself. Paying for her nursing services complicates the relationship.

On the way back down the stairs from El Castillo, Connor has to sit down on the steps and use his inhaler to open his airways. He is grateful that Lunaria manages to keep up a stream of bright chatter to distract him from his breathing difficulties. After fifteen minutes, he rises to his feet and tells her he is good to go on.

When they get back to La Rusa, Lunaria insists that Connor go to bed and rest. "While you sleep, I'll go back to the clinic. I offered to help out there for a couple of hours. They need help vaccinating the children," she tells him.

Connor feels beat. When he lies down, Lunaria pulls the sheet over him and adjusts the air conditioning before sitting on the bed next to him and reading a chapter of Carpentier's book. Connor falls asleep to the sensuous sound of Cuban Spanish. Lunaria closes the book, gets up carefully, kisses him on the forehead and lets herself out.

A far away sound of knocking causes Connor to swim back up to the surface of consciousness. The room is in darkness, the only sounds the faint drumming of the returning tide and the hum of the air conditioner. The knock comes again and he realizes someone is at the door. Can't be Lunaria. She has a key and, besides, the door is not usually locked.

"Come in. The door's open," he calls, his voice husky with sleep.

Suddenly silhouetted in the light from the hallway, Zoe. A rush of adrenalin brings Connor totally awake.

"Jesus!"

"Leaving without a word. You bastard! Is that all I mean to you?" Zoe steps inside and closes the door. Connor fumbles for a moment before finding the switch for the bedside lamp.

"Jesus! It's supposed to be all over between us, remember?"

"I found out about your illness and I had to come. God knows why but I kept thinking about the good times before..."

"Before you left me for a lesbian."

Zoe goes to sit on the other bed and stops herself. "Is this her bed or do you share?"

"Her room is next door. How'd you..."

"Never mind." She crosses and sits on the small chair beside the window. In the soft light, she looks like the Zoe he had married all those years ago. The faint smell of smoke tells him that she has just had a cigarette before seeking him out in the hotel. His penis, maybe because he has just awakened, is hard and Connor rolls over on his side to face her and to hide the tell-tale bump.

Frowning with anger, Zoe stares at him for a few moments.

"You're right," Connor says quickly. "I should have told you. It's just...it's just, well, I always hated calling you because whenever Aden answered she would be such a bitch and so..."

The frown fades away and her eyes well with tears. "Oh, Connor. I felt terrible when I found out. I left Aden the same night. I've been staying with Marnie."

Connor swings his legs onto the floor, keeping the sheet across his lap in an absurd attempt at modesty. "My God. Why do I still get so horny just looking at you?"

"Me too," she says, and moves on to the bed beside him. She lightly touches his erection through the sheet. "I'm glad you're pleased to see me."

As she quickly sheds her clothes and flings them on the chair, Connor risks a peek at the bedside alarm. After some anxious calculation, he figures they have at least an hour, probably more, before Lunaria gets back from the clinic.

They make love with as much passion as their first time. As he runs his hands over Zoe's body, all the questions buzzing around in his head and even the wheezing in his chest disappear and there is only her. "My God, Zoe, it's been such a long time."

"For me too."

When she cries out, Connor, whispering her name over and over, feels himself joining her in a few long moments of ecstasy.

"That probably woke the ghost," he tells her, and then has to begin explaining about Magdalena Rovenskaya.

Suddenly Zoe sits up. "Where's your *chica*?"

"Lunaria is working at the clinic near the *Colonial* but she should be home pretty soon." The realization makes him leap up and begin to dress. He is pulling on his pants and Zoe is looking frantically for her bra when the door quietly opens. Both stop and stand transfixed as they stare at Lunaria in her nurse's uniform, a look of shocked disbelief on her face. Time stands still for an instant and then, with an anguished cry, Lunaria is gone. Zoe flinches at the sound of the door slamming.

"Shit! Shit! Shit!" she says, shaking her head. "I didn't mean…"

"Of course not." The shock of Lunaria finding them together brings on a coughing fit and Connor has to sit on the bed for a couple of minutes. When he recovers, Zoe is dressed.

"Let's get out of here," she urges.

"I have to talk to her first. Why don't you go down to the bar and I'll see you in a few minutes." He continues dressing.

"Christ, I'm sorry."

"Go on. I'll be down in a little while."

When she has gone, Connor goes into the bathroom, stands in front of the mirror and forces himself to take a couple of fairly deep breaths. "You idiot," he tells his reflection as he reaches into his toilet kit and takes a couple of pills.

When he feels ready, he goes into the hall, and listens at Lunaria's door. Faint sounds could be Lunaria sobbing or maybe television noise. He raps softly. "Lunaria." No response. "Lunaria, I'm sorry. I didn't know she was coming."

No response.

He raps on the door again. "Lunaria."

"Go away." The voice is firm.

He considers knocking again but decides against it. "Let's talk in the morning. I'll see you then."

He waits a minute for a response but there is none so slowly he turns away and descends the stairs. Zoe is waiting in the bar.

"Let's get out of here," he says.

"Okay. I'll just finish my drink." Zoe swallows the last quarter of her Cuba libre and takes a last drag of her cigarette while Connor settles her bill.

"How about the Colonial?"

"Sure. I love that place."

As they step out into the light rain and turn up calle Ciro Frias, Connor remembers that the *Colonial* is two doors from the clinic where Lunaria works. "Maybe we'd better go up to Antonio Maceo. We can go to the Café el Patio. Remember it?"

"Where the band applauded us for doing a bolero. Connor,

of course I remember. One of the best places to dance in town."

"Yeah. Right. Don't think I'm up to that any more though."

Zoe can't think of anything to say so they walk in silence until they turn inland.

"How did you find me?" he asks, still mystified by Zoe's sudden appearance.

"Brenda said you'd gone to Cuba but I had already guessed. Your calendar in the kitchen had a note about the flight and there was a Hemingway book beside your bed."

"You went into my house?"

"I was worried about you. Okay? If you wanted to keep me out you should have moved the key. By the way, you should have got somebody to look after the place. I'm surprised the pipes didn't burst this winter."

"Andy said he'd be keeping an eye on it, like usual. I left the gas fire on low. I decided to come here in kind of a hurry." Instrumental music is coming from the Casa de trova. "Look, I'm tired. Let's stop in here. We can go to El Patio some other night."

"Sure. I wasn't even thinking."

"I won't break."

With the tourists gone, the place is almost deserted but the musicians seem not to mind. Zoe and Connor find a table in a corner. "Rum and coke?" Connor asks when the waiter comes.

"Yes."

"*Cuba libre y un mojito, por favor.*"

Over the next hour, she tells him about leaving Aden, about finding out just how sick Connor was, about her impulsive decision to look for him, and about the difficulty she had tracking down someone to look after her dance studio.

"But how did you know I was in Baracoa?"

"I need a cigarette."

"You can still smoke indoors in Cuba," he points out.

"I know but, you know, your condition."

"Go ahead. I'll let you know if it's bothering me."

"You're sure?"

He nods.

"Thanks." She lights her cigarette and carefully blows smoke towards the door. "I did a little detective work. If you were going to Cuba where would you stay? I decided that you would probably go to one of the *casas particulares* where we stayed when we were here."

"But I didn't."

"I know you didn't." Irritation colours her voice. "Anyway, I eliminated Havana and especially Santiago because of the pollution.

"Those diesel foggers for the mosquitoes nearly killed me. Funny the guide never mentioned the dengue fever problem there."

"Exactly. So I focused my search on Trinidad de Cuba and Baracoa."

"Because?"

"Clean air, and because you keep saying that they are two of the best places in the world."

"Oh, yeah."

"I emailed Maria Elena in Trinidad and said you were visiting Cuba and talked about staying with her again. She said you were welcome but so far she hadn't heard from you. I couldn't email Jacqui because she doesn't have a computer. So by process of elimination, I guessed you were here."

"At Jacqui's."

"Having seen your *chica*, I can see why you didn't stay with Jacqui."

"The cops check the *casas* much closer than the hotels. Anyway you found out where we were staying from Jacqui, right?"

"Right."

Zoe finishes her cuba libre and holds out her glass for another. The band is playing a slow version of "Bésame Mucho." When the waiter brings their fresh drinks, Zoe says, "Your turn. Who is she, your *chica*?"

"You didn't recognize her?"

The realization dawns slowly. "The nurse from the clinic? Nurse Boom-Boom?" He nods. "Oh my God, really? But how…"

"It's a long story." The four piece band is into the next set before he finishes.

For a moment, Zoe sits silent and then says quietly, "So you just called her and she agreed to your idea?"

Connor shrugs. "Not right away. We talked on the phone a lot."

"Her working as your nurse was your idea."

"Well, yeah. The cops here check for Cuban women staying with foreigners. The only way they'll leave you alone is if you register your relationship with the cops which can be tricky apparently. And, since there are so few foreigners in Baracoa, we stick out like a sore thumb."

"And you want to marry her so you can stay here until… Jesus, Connor do you know what you're doing?"

"Look, things were working out until you turned up," Connor counters with a flash of anger.

"You bastard! I put my life on hold for you." Rising, she hurries out onto the street. From his chair, Connor can see her back as she stands on the sidewalk. Her body language tells him she is very upset. He is still wondering whether to go to her when he sees her light a cigarette and walk away into the darkness. The band has stopped playing and are packing up their instruments. Connor checks his watch: just after midnight. He pays the tab and walks out into the light rain. The street is deserted at this time of night, out of season, so he has no trouble locating Zoe standing in a pool of light down near the v-shaped Plaza Independencia.

"Sorry. I'm really sorry," he says when he reaches her. He puts his hand on here shoulder and turns her towards him. She has been crying. "Oh, Zoe." He tries to embrace her but she pulls away.

"You should have called me."

"Yes, I should have. I just thought, you know, that it was all over. Christ, that's why I called Lunaria in the first place, otherwise…"

Suddenly they are clinging to each other. "I… I never stopped loving you," Zoe tells him.

"What about Aden?"

"Finished. Over. Done. More hero worship than anything else. I've been thinking a lot over the past few weeks since I found out how sick you were. You know, love is love. In the end that's all there is."

"Yes." Zoe can hear that he is having difficulty breathing.

"Sit here," she says and settles him on the edge of the high sidewalk. "I'm going down the street to find a bicitaxi."

He nods and she takes off at a run down the middle of the dark, deserted street. Still graceful as ever, he tells himself as he watches her. Now what do I do?

A few minutes later, a bicitaxi appears, a triumphant Zoe

sitting behind the driver. She helps him in and tells the driver to take them to the Hotel La Rusa.

The driver turns and looks at Connor. "You no looking good, man," he says.

Connor flashes a crooked smile, "Hi, Frank," he rasps. "Meet Zoe, my ex."

"Pleased to meet you, Frank," she tells him and adds, "He needs to get to the hotel."

Looking puzzled, Frank nods and begins pumping his powerful legs. "He used to be a boxer," Connor manages. "Good guy."

"Don't talk. Just lean on me." She puts her arm around him and tries to cushion him from the jolts. "Feeling any better?"

"Yes," Connor lies.

Turning down calle Frank País, they pass Jacqui's place. "That's where I'm staying," Zoe tells Connor.

"That was my guess."

Silence for a few moments, then Zoe asks, "Have you asked her to marry you?"

"Lunaria? No. But I think I am going to."

"So you could stay on in Baracoa?"

"Something like that. Can you think of a better place to live?"

She ignored the question. "And why would she marry you?"

"Money, Canadian citizenship?" After a pause, he adds, "Love?"

"And now?"

"Now. I have no idea what happens next. Your coming has scrambled my master plan." Hurriedly he adds, "But hey, my heart almost stopped when I saw you standing in the doorway to my room. Look, it wasn't just because I didn't want to speak to Aden that I didn't call. I...I couldn't bring myself to say

goodbye, you know. God knows I'll be saying goodbye soon
enough…"

Zoe held him for the rest of the ride, convinced at last
that she had been right to come. "You'll be okay?" she asks as
Frank helps Connor out of the bicitaxi.

"Yeah."

"What are you going to say to Lunaria?"

"I wish I knew."

Without being asked, Frank tells Zoe, "I'll help him up to
his room."

"That would be great, Frank," she tells him. "Then you can
drive me home."

When he reaches his door, Connor thanks Frank and
waits until he hears Frank's steps reach the next landing before
tiptoeing over to Lunaria's door and pressing his ear against it.
Sounds emanating from the television. Maybe she is awake.
He hesitates, wondering whether to knock, finally deciding to
wait until the morning.

The next morning begins with a loud knock on his door.
Without waiting for him to respond, Lunaria enters and
salutes him with a cheerful "*Buenos dias, Señor* Connor." She
is wearing her white nurse's uniform.

"*Buenos dias*, Lunaria."

"Time for your medicines before breakfast," she says
briskly. "I have written out a daily regimen for you to follow that
includes medication times and at least two hours of exercise."

"Look, Lunaria, ah, *discúlpeme, lo siento mucho,*" says
Connor hoping the Spanish is correct.

"No need to apologize. I'm just your nurse, right?"

"That was Zoe you saw last night. Believe me I was as surprised as you were."

"I doubt that, *Señor* Connor." She comes out of the bathroom with a bottle of water and four different pills for him to take.

"Lunaria, can we drop the '*señor*'?"

"You're the boss."

"Oh, for Christ sake!"

"I'll be next door if you need me."

"Lunaria, wait…" but she is gone.

When he goes down for breakfast, he has the small covered patio to himself. Can't blame Lunaria, he tells himself. Or Zoe for that matter. When he has finished his *café con leche* and still no sign of Lunaria, he decides to walk down the Malecón to try to figure out what to do. One thing he is pleased about: his breathing has definitely improved. Tango is waiting for him as usual.

"Just a moment." A muffled voice behind the hotel room door. Zoe has already tried Connor's door but now she is waiting nervously outside Lunaria's room. A minute later Lunaria appears in her crisp, white nurse's uniform. She mutters something that might be a Cuban curse and begins to shut the door.

Zoe pushes it open. "You and I have to talk," she tells Lunaria as she steps into her room. "I'd rather not do it here. I saw Connor walking away down the Malecón as I turned the corner. He might be back any time and I think we need to talk alone."

"What is there to say?" says Lunaria.

"Look, get dressed, unless you want to play nurse." For a moment the two women stared at each other. "Come on. We don't have much time."

Without a word but still keeping her eyes on the much

taller Zoe, Lunaria changes into a light summer dress with a floral pattern and high-heeled sandals. As they are about to emerge from the hotel, Zoe gestures for Lunaria to wait while she peers down the seawall in the direction Connor had taken. No sign of him.

Neither woman says a word until they reach the relative bustle of Antonio Maceo. Zoe leads the way to an open air café just off the Plaza Independencia. They take a table near the street with a good view of the old church. Zoe notices that the cathedral is still under repair but much has been done since her last visit. Not until they order *cafés con leche* does Zoe light a cigarette and begin to speak.

"I'm Zoe, Lunaria, but you probably already figured that out." She waits for a moment but Lunaria makes no attempt to fill the silence. "I can't tell you how sorry I am about yesterday."

"Is not my business."

"Oh, yes it is. Look, whatever you think about me, I came down here because I was worried about him, not to restart our relationship."

"Really?" says Lunaria. "You two seemed to be getting along well last night."

Zoe sighed. "Look. It just happened. You know we used to be married." Lunaria glares at her but says nothing. "I swear I'm no threat to you."

"Connor is my patient and…"

"Oh, it's pretty obvious he's way more than that. He's thinking of asking you to marry him. Did you know that?"

Lunaria's expression softens a little. "He told you that?"

"Not in so many words but it was pretty clear."

"But then you arrive and immediately you are in bed with him. What am I to make of that?"

Zoe, feeling herself getting emotional, takes a drag from her cigarette and hesitates while the waiter puts down their coffees before saying, "I still love him, you know. I'm here to help. Last night was a one time thing." She glances at Lunaria who is still looking skeptical. "Look, I swear it will not happen again. He needs you, Lunaria. I'm here to help in any way I can. Last night I saw just how sick he is…" She stops and takes a deep drag on her cigarette. Usually, the nicotine helps calm her, prevent the tears, but not this time. "He wants to end it here with you. I won't interfere and I'll help all I can. So please…I need you to forgive me for last night."

For a moment, Lunaria says nothing as she feels her anger draining away. Finally she takes a deep breath and puts her hand over Zoe's. "I'm sure he's glad you came. And, for me, it will be nice to have another woman to talk to."

Zoe goes on to tell Lunaria about her relationship with Aden. Far from being shocked at the news that Zoe is a lesbian, Lunaria is full of questions which Zoe readily answers.

"But last night you were…"

"In bed with Connor? Yes. As I told Connor, love is love. I still feel love for Aden, although I can't stand her most of the time. At the same time, I never stopped loving Connor. Does that make sense?"

For an answer, Lunaria rises, comes around the table and hugs Zoe, giving her a kiss on the cheek. "Welcome to Baracoa," she says in Zoe's ear.

When they get back to Hotel La Rusa, Connor is sitting in the bar morosely sipping a mojito. "We've come to an agreement," Zoe announces. "We'll both be here for you but I'm only here to help Lunaria."

"What?"

"You're stuck with both of us."

Throughout the heat and the sudden storms of the rainy season, *los tres amigos*, as they christened themselves, have become inseparable. Most nights, when Connor is feeling all right, they go to the Café el Patio located in a building that had been severely damaged during Hurricane Ike. Much of the ceiling collapsed but, through some miracle, the roof still keeps out the rain. The temporary ceiling that Connor and Zoe sat under on the last visit has been repaired and draped with camo netting. The tables and chairs are the same uncomfortable wrought iron designs found all over Cuba and the lighting is primitive but the feel of the place overcomes all shortcomings. Admission is one peso and after their fourth or fifth visit, Valeria, the woman on the door, begins to greet them warmly by name, refuse the payment and wave them in.

For the past couple of days, there had been only one topic of conversation throughout this isolated town, the tropical storm two hundred kilometres off the coast of eastern Cuba. Already signs of preparation are everywhere and the government is warning the residents of Baracoa to be ready to evacuate across the mountains.

Lately Connor has been depressed by his slowly deteriorating health and the two women have had difficulty getting him to leave the hotel. Now all that has changed.

"It's the hurricane," Zoe tells Lunaria.

"*Sí*. It's all he's talked about since the news came on the television."

"Yeah. This morning, after you left for the clinic, I found

him sitting in the bar drinking coffee. He had spread the pages of the *Granma* across the table and covered them with pieces of cameras. He was cleaning and checking his lenses and the two camera bodies he brought with him. 'Only wish I'd brought some video equipment,' he told me. Oh, and he is kicking himself for not bringing a laptop with his Photoshop software on it."

"It's given him, oh, you know..."

"Something to live for? Yeah, I thought of that."

"How does he think he'll get the pictures out of Cuba?"

"I think he was hoping that you could help him with that."

"In Havana, maybe. But here? I don't think so. And the government will probably order us evacuated over the mountains to Santiago so he will not get his pictures anyway."

Zoe puts her arm around Lunaria and says, "If he asks just say you'll see what you can do, okay? No sense raining on his parade. He's been so happy the last little while."

"Okay."

Zoe kisses her on the cheek. "Great. Now, d'you think we can drag him out to Café el Patio, tonight?"

Lunaria smiles and says, "Count on it."

For some time now, *los tres amigos* have been the only patrons at the Café el Patio who are not native Baracoans. Tonight, a Wednesday, there is a buzz running through the crowd as the conga players begin laying down their salsa rhythms. Today the tropical storm has been upgraded to a hurricane and given the name 'Linda'. The first storm of the season to intensify into a hurricane, Linda has begun to track west and is currently predicted to make landfall to the east of them in Haiti. But the path of a hurricane is unpredictable and Baracoa is only about 150 kilometres from the tip of Haiti.

The Café el Patio is full tonight, unusual for a Wednesday, especially at this time of year. The atmosphere is electric as people celebrate as if there will be no tomorrow; perhaps for some, there won't be.

"Must have been like this during World War II just before the Germans entered Paris," Connor says.

"People are keyed up, that's for sure," Zoe agrees.

During the first set, Raúl, one of the Afro-Cubans who has become a friend, comes over and, as is the custom, asks Connor's permission to dance with Zoe. When she arrived in Cuba the first time, she had never danced salsa or son but with a dancer's body memory she learned the steps to both with ease. The hip action that is second nature to Cubanas took a little longer to perfect. The Café el Patio attracts the best dancers in town but whenever Zoe, tall and slim, steps on to the darkened dance floor all eyes are on her.

"Aren't they amazing together," Connor says to Lunaria.

"Amazing. Raúl is great but Zoe, Zoe is magic," says Lunaria.

As they whirl, other dancers move aside to watch. One of the conga players brings his drum to the edge of the low stage and begins to spur on the dancers with sudden bursts of complicated salsa rhythms. Raúl and Zoe respond. Both look cool despite the heat of the evening. As the drummer reaches a frenzy, Raúl tosses Zoe towards him. She spins in the air, lands on the stage in her high heels, does a back-bend and slams the drum with her the back of her hand to wild applause. As Raúl returns Zoe to her table, Mikael, the lead singer, jumps down lightly from the stage, whisks two cold beers off a passing tray and hands one to each of them.

For the next hour or so, the two women chat to each other leaving Connor to watch the band and the dancers. He is remembering better times when he had the energy to dance with Zoe. If you want to look good on the dance floor, Connor muses to himself, make sure you have a talented partner.

But now, here he is, watching the passing parade but, as Hurricane Linda approaches, he feels that the storm is lifting him out of the depression he has been wallowing in.

"...I swear she had had so many facelifts that she couldn't close her eyes," Zoe is telling Lunaria, "and, would you believe a wooden leg, but dammit that woman had an instinct for dance that was positively uncanny. Maybe it was the Russian training, I don't know but she was amazing. She was my 'La Rusa'. Taught me to stop counting and to let myself dance."

"Some people just find the perfect role in their journey through life," comments Lunaria. "Alexei was Russian and, believe me, he couldn't dance a step."

"True," acknowledges Zoe, remembering Lunaria's stories about her ex. "Hey, where you going?" she asks Connor as he rises and crosses to the stage. He just waves to her. At his signal, Mikael leans down. Connor whispers in his ear and the singer nods, turns to the band and says, "Bolero."

Connor, smiling, turns and holds his hand out to Zoe. "Finally dark enough to dance," he tells her.

Zoe, suppresses the urge to tell him that perhaps he should conserve his strength. "I'd love to," she tells him and they glide out on to the floor. The bolero is more slow and sensual than athletic so they dance as if there is only this moment. Beyond the building, the rumbling of distant thunder adds a basso register to the beat. "Dance is one of the greatest gifts you ever gave me," he tells her as she passes back and forth in front of him in a move known as the sliding doors.

She spins and they sidestep together as she says, "You have

been the greatest love of my life. Not until you got so ill did I realize it."

"Too late?"

"Never too late." Her eyes are glistening with tears. "Before I came I looked up your illness on the net. Many people have just got better. No one knows why. If we had access to the internet here, I could show you."

"I love you," he tells her as the music ends and the rest of the small crowd applauds the Canadians. The band strikes up a cha-cha as they get back to the table.

"You look so good together," Lunaria tells her.

"Come on," Zoe says grabbing Lunaria's hand, "Let's show him how his *chicas* cha-cha."

For a couple of minutes, Connor watches, delighted, as the women whirl but he feels the familiar tightness in his chest, the usual precursor to a severe coughing fit. Rising slowly, he feels his way slowly back to the only bathroom in the place. The older woman with the strange black wig who guards the door stops him as someone is already inside. Connor nods and leans against the wall. The tightness, like a band across his chest, makes his breathing shallow. He tries his inhaler but it gives little relief.

"Is okay." The voice of the woman who guards the door.

Connor looks up to see a stunning Afro-Cuban woman dressed all in white pass him on the way back to the dance floor. He nods and drops a peso coin in the saucer on the older woman's table. Inside he leans heavily on the sink and looks at himself in the cracked mirror. "You look terrible," he mutters looking at the pallor in the mirror and the beads of sweat standing out on his forehead. "Anybody'd think you were dying." He tries a smile but is panting too hard. Just like the day he had met Lunaria in the clinic in Havana, he feels himself growing faint, the lights growing dim. Concentrate on something, he tells himself. He looks over at the toilet. No seat of course and the cracked cistern is still held together with a coat hanger. Must be a story behind that...

"Connor! Connor!"

He opens his eyes to see three women staring down at him: the washroom attendant, Zoe and Lunaria.

"Feeling any better?" Zoe asks anxiously as the bicitaxi stops at Hotel La Rusa.

"Yeah," he says automatically, but his voice has all but gone. He decides to be honest. "No. This is the worst yet."

Lunaria's bicitaxi has arrived first and the two women support Connor as he fights for breath climbing the stairs. When they reach his room, Lunaria rushes ahead and arranges pillows so that he can sit up. After helping her get Connor on to the bed, Zoe stands back while Lunaria takes charge, forcing pills into Connor with gulps of cold bottled water and fussing with the sheets. When Connor closes his eyes and begins to breathe more regularly, Lunaria tells Zoe to go down to the bar and have a cigarette. When Zoe begins to protest, Lunaria adds, "When you come up, you can watch him while I get some sleep. Bring me a daiquiri when you come up, oh, and some more bottled water for Connor."

Zoe sees the logic of her argument, nods and descends the stairs. Shortly after eleven, she is the only customer in the bar. "Is he going to be all right?" asks Abelardo who is the night man this week.

"I wish I knew," Zoe tells him before lighting a cigarette and ordering a Cuba libre for herself. She sits at the bar as the winds have picked up outside. At about midnight Zoe orders a daiquiri and a couple of cold bottles of ice water and goes back up to Connor's room.

"He is sleeping," Lunaria whispers as Zoe comes in.

Handing her the daiquiri, Zoe gives her a gentle hug. "You're marvellous," she tells Lunaria.

To Zoe's surprise, Lunaria carefully puts down her daiquiri and returns the hug. "The way you dance," Lunaria sighs into her ear, "magic."

Zoe kisses her cheek and whispers, "Thanks."

Lunaria hesitates for a moment and then kisses Zoe on the lips. "I have been thinking of doing that for the last two weeks," she says.

"Really? Me too, but you already knew that about me."

Lunaria grins, sips her daiquiri and they kiss again. Zoe can taste the rum. "Do you think it would be all right if I stayed over. I don't like to walk back to Jacqui's place with Connor like this."

"My room," says Lunaria immediately. "I've given him something that should let him sleep till the morning. Come on."

One after the other, the women kiss Connor lightly on the forehead and tiptoe out of the room.

The next morning, they check on Connor and find him still sleeping soundly, his breathing regular. "Let's have some breakfast and then see if he's woken up," says Zoe.

"Sleep is the best thing for him," Lunaria agrees.

At breakfast the news is all about the coming evacuation. Hurricane Linda has turned towards the eastern coast of Cuba and could arrive within the next twenty-four hours. The waiter tells them that the authorities are already rounding up vehicles to evacuate the people of Baracoa across the mountains to Santiago.

"Jesus!" exclaims Zoe. "Our last stay in Santiago almost killed Connor. You know they have machines to generate clouds of diesel smoke to keep down the mosquitoes that carry dengue fever? I could hardly breathe, never mind him. Connor was sick for a week. That's how we met you at that clinic in Havana. We can't take Connor to Santiago. Out of the question."

"But staying here will be very dangerous," Lunaria objects.

"We'll move up to El Castillo. At least, we won't get flooded out up there."

"But the winds. I'm scared Zoe."

Zoe puts her arm around Lunaria and says. "You'd be crazy not to be. I'm scared too but moving Connor to Santiago in his condition will kill him. Look, you stay here with him and I'll go up and see if I can get us rooms.

"Okay," Lunaria agrees.

Zoe can see that Lunaria is still uneasy and adds, "It'll work out. You'll see."

Lunaria nods. Rising, and checking that Maritsa, the server this morning, is not watching, Zoe leans over and kisses Lunaria on the lips. "We're going to be all right."

"Yes. We'll all be fine. Go and get us a place to stay."

Yesterday the only clouds in the sky had been thin bands of stratus but today everything has changed. The lowering cumulus clouds are brick red with dust blown all the way from Africa but the air is still, still and very hot. The sea, however, is flinging waves over the breakwater on to the Malecón. No children are playing there today.

"He's sleeping," she tells Tango. The little dog is sitting beside the back door waiting for his walk with Connor. Zoe pets him and sets off away from the sea through the Plaza Marti. Looking back she sees that Tango has not moved.

Everywhere she looks people are installing storm shutters, putting away chairs, tables, and anything else that might become a projectile. She notes as she passes that the women are still working at the cigar factory. When she reaches Frank País, she turns back towards the sea and Jacqui's *casa*.

"I was worried when you didn't come back last night," Jacqui scolds as Zoe walks in the open door. "Here, help me."

"Sorry, but Connor got very sick and I stayed over at La Rusa," Zoe tells her as she hands the small portable stereo wrapped in plastic up to Jacqui. Jacqui, who is standing on a chair, wraps it in towels and places it carefully on top of a cupboard. She gets down and says, "Let's have some coffee."

They enjoy a *café con leche* together sitting in front of the tiny television and watch the reports on Hurricane Linda. "The TV is the last thing I'm going to pack before we go up to Plaza Independencia. That's where the buses are leaving from."

"I can't go," Zoe tells her.

"But everyone has to go. The government has given the order."

"Connor's too sick to travel. I'm on my way up to El Castillo to try to get rooms there."

"But…" She stops and looks at Zoe for a moment. "Make sure you get rooms on the south side looking towards El Yunque."

"Thanks."

For the next hour, Zoe packs her own suitcase and then helps Jacqui pack up the dishes and wrap her souvenirs. Jacqui manages to hold it together until she picks up the plastic cylinder with the tiny statue of the Virgin of the Copper. Clutching it in her hand, she sinks on to a chair and begins to weep. Zoe holds her but there is nothing to say. A few minutes later, with an almost heroic effort, Jacqui gets to her feet and, still clutching her souvenir, says, "The virgin will help us. You'll see."

Zoe nods, too moved to say anything. As she leaves Jacqui, she tells her that she will be back in an hour or two to pick up her suitcase. Jacqui tells her that if she has already gone, the suitcase will be just inside the door. Zoe doesn't need to ask if the door will be locked. No one in Baracoa locks their doors.

Zoe is surprised to find the courtyard of Hotel El Castillo is packed with people. Workmen are beginning to drain the pool as she pushes through the crowd chiding herself for not staying with Connor and letting Lunaria arrange the hotel. Soon five or six old cars, their gears whining from the steep climb, emerge into the small turnaround behind the hotel and the crowd begins to thin out. She realizes that the few guests and most of the staff are being evacuated.

She stops a woman in a maid's uniform and says, "*Donde es el...* ah, hotel manager, *por favor.*"

"*Que?*"

"*El jefe del hotel,*" she tries, suspecting that '*jefe*' is not the right word but hoping the maid will understand the link.

"Ah, *el gerente,*" she takes Zoe's hand and leads her to a small balding man, leaning over the pool and issuing orders to the workmen.

"*Muchas gratias,*" Zoe tells her and turns to the manager. "*Perdón.*"

At first he ignores her but she refuses to go away. At the fourth try, he turns to tell her he is busy when he recognizes her and says, "Ah, *señora* Zoe. What can I do for you?"

Despite almost constant interruptions from people needing the manager's attention, Zoe manages to tell her story. When she is finished, he tells her the three of them will have to share a room as the hotel is being used to house people too frail and infirm to make the trip to Santiago. Zoe thanks him and hurries back to the stairs.

Heading down the stairs to the town, she notes that the wind has picked up and the clouds are beginning to scud across the sky. From the top of the steps she can see the yellow building that is Hotel La Rusa to her right and beyond it the sea crashing over the seawall.

On the way back to the hotel, Zoe has to avoid *Plaza Independencia* as it is blocked by a crowd of people waiting patiently to board the buses that are beginning to arrive from Santiago. On one of the benches, She spots Frank who is passing around a bottle of rum with two other bicitaxi drivers as they watch a chess game. When she gets back to La Rusa, she finds that Lunaria has already packed for both herself and Connor. "Connor is downstairs eating," Lunaria tells her.

"You think he's strong enough to walk all the way up to El Castillo?"

"If we take our time."

"Look, I just saw Frank. Let me see if I can get him to take Connor up," Zoe tells her.

"That would be great," Lunaria tells her.

Twenty minutes later, Zoe turns up at the door of the hotel in the back of Frank's bicitaxi.

"Wait here, Frank," she tells him. "I'll be back in a couple of minutes."

She finds Connor in his usual place at the second table. "I've got you a ride up to El Castillo," she tells him.

"I can walk," he protests.

"Not with your luggage. Come on. It's settled."

She hustles him out to the bicitaxi. When Frank sees him,

his battered face breaks into a crooked grin. "I'm your ride, *amigo*," he tells Connor who breaks into a smile, shaking his head.

"These women…"

"They look after you," says Frank. "Me too, *amigo*. Climb up."

A few minutes later, Zoe and Lunaria appear with Connor's suitcase and heave it in beside him. They each kiss him and promise to see him at the top of the hill.

"We may have to walk up that final hill," says Frank. "It's very steep and if the rains catch us…"

"If anything happens, just wait for us," says Lunaria.

Frank laughs and hammers down on the pedals, "We'll be all right. You women look after yourselves," he says as he turns up towards town.

The women wave until the bicitaxi passes out of sight and then hug each other.

"I'm scared," Lunaria tells Zoe.

Zoe tries to smile. "So am I," she says finally and kisses her companion before saying suddenly, "Tango! We should take him too. You know how he loves Connor."

For ten minutes before they go upstairs to get Lunaria's luggage, the women scour the neighbourhood for the black dog but there is no sign of him. "He's probably found a safe place to hide from the storm," says Lunaria, at last. Zoe nods and they climb the slippery, irregular marble steps to their room to collect Lunaria's suitcase and shoulder bag.

By the time Frank threads his way through the town and begins to ascend the winding road, the winds have picked up and a sudden squall drenches him and his passenger despite the plastic curtains around the rear seat. Rain is already creating rivers running down the road and, after a supreme effort, Frank can go no farther. "We will have to walk, *amigo*," he tells Connor. Connor nods as Frank puts a powerful arm around his shoulders and grabs his suitcase with the other hand. "How you feelin'?" Frank asks him as they start up, rain driving into their faces.

"Still bobbing and weaving, *amigo*, still on my feet."

Frank laughs. "Then we can go the distance."

An hour later the two women, tired and wet, finally make the last of the steps and pause, breathless, in the breezeway, out of the rain. And there is Connor sitting on his suitcase, fast asleep. No sign of Frank. They waken Connor and are shown to a stuffy, airless room. The window that would normally give a view of El Yunque has been boarded up so they turn on a bedside lamp and half carry the exhausted Connor to the bed nearest to the bathroom.

"At least we still have electricity," Lunaria says.

"Oh, yeah. It's going to be pretty dark in here if we have a blackout."

When we have a blackout, thinks Lunaria but says, "I'll see if I can get some candles."

"I need a cigarette," Zoe tells her, "and maybe I'll see if I can buy some food at the *mercado*. The rain's stopping. I'll be back at soon as I can." Zoe returns before dark with four packs of Hollywood cigarettes for herself and two packages of biscuits. "It's all I could find," she tells Lunaria.

"I got a candle from the front desk," says Lunaria. "We'll be fine."

That night they spend watching television in their room. The radar images of the approaching storm terrify them both as they huddle together on the other bed. Connor wakes about eleven and tells them he's feeling much stronger. As if to prove it, he begins to rummage around in his suitcase.

"What are you looking for?" Lunaria asks.

"My cameras."

"Here. Let me get them. Otherwise I'll have to repack." Lunaria unzips a side compartment and hands him his two Nikon SLR's. "There."

"It'll be too dangerous to go out there anyway," Zoe tells him.

"I know, I know," says Connor, irritated.

"Okay, okay. No need to get mad."

The hurricane hits with full force just before dawn. The roar of the winds around the hotel is punctuated by unexplained crashes, sounds of breaking glass and the occasional scream. At one point a tremendous cracking sound as part of the roof facing the sea is ripped to pieces, followed by a clattering of red tiles smashing on the deck outside. A few minutes later the power suddenly dies as a line snaps somewhere. Lunaria borrows Zoe's lighter and lights their single candle. Cries of "*¡Socorro!*" Help! and "*¡Médico!*" are coming from the seaward side of the hotel.

"I have to go and see if I can help," Lunaria tells Zoe and Connor.

"I'll come with you," Zoe tells her. "At least I know a little first aid."

"Will you be all right, Connor?"

"Sure. In fact, I'm feeling way better than at any time in the past twenty-four hours," he says, standing up and stretching. "Maybe I could help."

"No, no. You must stay here," Lunaria tells him sternly.

"But I..."

"Listen to your nurse!" says Zoe.

When the women leave, Connor checks out his cameras making sure they have plenty of battery life before putting them in their waterproof cases and strapping one across each side of his chest. He peers out the door. The corridor is empty. He listens for a moment. Something is missing. What is it? The express-train roar of the wind. It's time.

Connor hurries outside. The winds have abated but are still considerable. The torrential rains, too, have slackened off. His first shot is of a wild scattering of red tiles that have blown off the roof. He looks to the south: El Yunque is completely obscured by dark, roiling clouds. Thunder crashes and lightning puncture the darkness that blankets Baracoa even though the sun came up more than three hours ago.

At the top of the steps, he pulls out one of his cameras and begins shooting rapidly. When the women left, Connor had only planned to come here to the railing overlooking the town but suddenly a strange thing happens. The rain stops abruptly and the wind drops to almost nothing. A single patch of sunlight illuminates the eastern end of the seafront. The mustard yellow walls of Hotel La Rusa glow in the unexpected shaft of light. Looking up Connor sees a parabola of blue sky. I'll never get a better chance, he tells himself and begins to descend the steps. The calm holds as he reaches the bottom and heads down a side street of houses painted in green, yellow or pink pastels. As he reaches Antonio Maceo, he turns right towards Plaza Independencia. A brown horse with wild eyes gallops towards him and he fires off several shots in rapid succession, catching the creature's wild eyes and the flecks of foam at its mouth. Then he dives into a doorway as it skids in front of him, gathers itself and gallops on. He walks a little farther and sees that the wrought iron fence around the outdoor café on the plaza is buckled and a mangled bicitaxi is embedded in its twisted bars. Connor looks at it closely and is relieved that it is not Frank's.

He sits for a few minutes on the steps of the café and leans back against the locked gate. After a while, his panting decreases and he notices that the town is eerily quiet.

Heaving himself to his feet, Connor decides to take calle Frank País, the street that contains Jacqui's *casa.*

"Have you seen Connor?" There is a note of panic in Zoe's voice.

"No, why?" Lunaria does not even look up as she dabs iodine on the cuts an old man received when part of the roof collapsed.

"He's gone."

"What?"

"I've just been to the room. No sign of him."

Lunaria hands the bottle of iodine to the woman who has been assisting her and says, "Are all Canadian men so crazy?"

The women run out on to the patio and cross to the steps down into town. No sign of him. "At least the wind has dropped," Zoe says. "I'm going down to look for him."

"No!" shouts Lunaria. "Look." She points up at the small patch of blue high above the encircling clouds. "We're in the eye of the storm. It will be back soon."

Zoe heads for the steps. Over her shoulder, she says, "I've got to try."

With surprising speed, Lunaria lunges and grabs her. "I can't let you go. I can't lose both of you."

Zoe struggles for a moment before going limp. She turns back to Lunaria. "You don't think he has a chance."

"Oh, he'll probably find shelter. In fact, I'd bet on it. But the chances of finding him after the storm hits again…" She shrugs.

As the wind begins to pick up once more, the sky darkens. If Connor were to look up at El Castillo, he might see the two women clinging together, comforting each other over his disappearance, but he is already up to his knees in the sea water that has rushed up the streets and into many of the houses. He turns down the street above the Malecón and passes the bakery and an old car balanced crazily on two wheels against a lamppost. Only last week, he and Lunaria had chatted to the man who was lovingly repainting it. Even now, scraps of newspaper are still stuck to its windows, glued there by the green paint the man had used.

As the wind starts to scream again, Connor finds himself on the leeward side of the Hotel La Rusa. "Must have been drawn to it," he says to himself. The sea is once again sending huge standing waves across the seawall and the road to slam into the houses along the seafront. The door to the hotel is hanging at an odd angle. "Got to get out of this," he tells himself. At the moment he is protected from the full fury of the sea by the hotel itself but, as each fresh waves comes in, the water rises up to his waist and then tries to drag him towards the shore as it recedes. Connor is about to retreat into the relative safety of the hotel when he spies Tango swimming towards him, being buffeted from side to side by the huge waves. Connor waits for an opportune moment and lunges for the little dog, managing to grab a single hind leg. The dog whimpers in protest but Connor pulls him in, tucks him under his arm, and pushes into the hotel.

The whole building seems to be shaking as wave after wave crashes into the façade on the other side. The noise is incredible and Connor finds it terrifying and exhilarating at the same time. He wades past the desk still carrying Tango who has started to lick his cheek. "Hey, *perro negro*, cut it out," he tells the dog but it just wags its sopping tail.

It is so gloomy in the hotel now that Connor has to peer closely and feel his way until he finds the steps up to the rooms. The climb is hard and Connor discovers that almost all of his strength has left him. Dragging himself up the first flight of steps, he feels his heart thumping. Even the little dog becomes an unbearable weight and he puts Tango down on the stairs. The dog bounds up ahead of him and waits on the landing. "Six steps," he whispers as he rests in the middle of the flight, "seven more to go."

With the last of his strength, Connor reaches the first floor landing. He knows he cannot make another flight and starts to wonder why he is heading for his old room anyway. "Because it's home now," he mutters, then cursing his weakness he drops his cameras and sinks to the floor. Tango, shivering, climbs into his lap. Even here water is running over the floor and trickling down the steps. "Seas coming in the windows," Connor guesses. There is a tightness in his chest again as the seas pound the hotel relentlessly and the whole world seems ready to tumble down. Absentmindedly, he pets the wet dog and stares vacantly into the darkness of the hallway. There in front of him, scarcely visible, the ghostly figure of a woman is dancing to the rhythms of the wind. He recognizes Mima

Rubenskaya, smiles, and gently puts the dog aside. When she beckons to him, he joins the dance.

∽

When they had first moved into Connor's house, Zoe and Lunaria felt as if they were engulfed by his presence: his photographs, his books, his equipment, his winter clothes, even the contents of his medicine cabinet. True, Connor had willed the place to Lunaria, a will he must have drawn up before he left for Cuba, but it took the better part of a year before they were able to give his clothes away, and pack most of his books and pictures. The next summer they held a yard sale to get rid of much of the rest of Connor's stuff. The proceeds they sent to a fund for Baracoa Hurricane Relief. The sale raised only a few hundred dollars, but when added to the money they had raised from the sale of Connor's pictures of the devastation the sum for disaster relief was considerable.

At long last, the women are beginning to feel that they are making the house their own.

Recovering from the sight of the devastation in Baracoa after the hurricane is still an ongoing process. Some nights Lunaria still has nightmares about one woman that she could not save. Zoe had spotted Jacqui getting off one of the buses that had just returned from Santiago and accompanied her to her *casa* on Frank País. When they got there, the door was split in two by the seas that had thundered up the street. One look into the livingroom and Jacqui had collapsed to her knees.

Frank had disappeared, his body never found, but of course the greatest blow to Zoe and Lunaria had been the news of Connor's fate. Rescuers had discovered his body the day after Hurricane Linda had bounced back out to sea and eventually blown itself out over southern Nova Scotia. There was still no electricity in the town when two of the Cuban military sent by Raúl Castro had penetrated the Hotel La Rusa. Shining their flashlights into the dark hallway, they saw a figure propped against the wall staring into the darkness. Beside him, a small black dog sat like a sentinel. When he saw them the dog began to whine softly. One of the soldiers searched his pack. When he found his lunch, he offered half a sandwich to the dog.

"Poor little thing's starving," said his companion as the dog quickly ate the food.

"He's been guarding the body all this time," said the first.

The story of Tango's heroism was first printed in the *Granma* newspaper before being picked up by the wire services and spread across the internet. For a few shining moments, Tango became one of the world's most famous canines.

Connor had wanted to be buried in Cuba, but as Lunaria had warned the bureaucracy would make it impossible to carry out his wish. As a result Zoe arranged to transport the body back to Sudbury. Lunaria was allowed an exit visa. Zoe still claims that her forthcoming marriage to Connor was the reason but Lunaria thinks that Tango's heroism made the government look on her application favourably.

On the anniversary of Connor's death Zoe and Lunaria put Tango in their car and drive the short distance to a tiny cemetery carved out of the bush at the very end of Skead Road, which leads to the airport. There they lay flowers on his grave and reminisce about *los tres amigos* and their time in Baracoa.

Tango sits quietly and stares at the small headstone. The women head back to the car before realizing that the black dog is not with them. They turn back and see Tango, a silent sentinel, still sitting next to Connor's grave.

RIDING TO CAMBODIA

Nine Thai monks. In single file with our alms bowls, we set out as soon as the sun has brightened enough to make out the lines on a man's hand. Since I have been permitted to go on the alms rounds, this has been my favourite time of day. The mists rise and swirl along the river; the birds congratulate each new day, and the still waters in the terraced rice paddies, like shards of a shattered mirror, reflect the crimson sky. Today the first people that we meet are a mother and her three children. Bowing with hands together in a wai of great respect, they dole out parcels of sticky rice wrapped in banana leaves. When my turn comes, one of the little boys looks up at me and whispers, "*Fra Farang*," foreign brother. I suppress a smile and accept his offering with all the humility I possess.

My road from Northern Ontario to this Buddhist monastery in Northern Thailand has been a winding one to say the least. One of my earliest memories is of dressing in my hooded bathrobe and solemnly blessing my siblings much to the delight of my agnostic father and the disgust of my devout Irish mother. The fact that I was only imitating the Grey Friar who had visited our church the previous Sunday had not saved me from her beating. Not surprisingly, my interest in religion had faded after that, and by my teenage years I had given it up entirely. When I learned in university that my favourite writer, Joseph Conrad, had called Christianity "an absurd oriental myth" my views had been confirmed.

So when I returned to Thailand almost two years ago now, I had not come to seek a spiritual awakening. Far from it. I had been drawn back to the Land of Smiles for the first time in twenty years hoping to recapturing the freewheeling days of my youth in Bangkok. Call it, middle-age crazy.

Last time, I had flown in from Perth, Australia, with my best buddy Trent. That had been my second visit to Thailand, Trent's fifth or sixth. This time I had come in on a one-way ticket determined to stay. My nine hour flight from Sydney had arrived just after five in the morning.

The elevated four-lane into downtown Bangkok was new and depressingly North American. Very little traffic that early in the morning until we descended into the tangle of streets. I smiled as I glimpsed the Chao Phraya River over to the right as we entered the China Town district. "Gold Street," said the driver as we turned towards my hotel. "Still looks the same," I said, a surge of excitement overcoming my jet lag. He nodded as I looked out at the shuttered gold shops.

Past a fountain, he turned into the hotel's covered drop off point and stopped. Even before I paid the driver, a uniformed doorman opened the taxi door, flashed me one of those famous Thai smiles and said, "Welcome to the Grand China Princess, sir." A porter wheeled over one of those brass hotel trolleys that seem to permeate the world's hotels and began loading my luggage. A lifetime of traveling made me reluctant to turn my back on my bags, but then I had only rarely traveled at this level of luxury. Here, I had to remind myself, there was no need to worry. The spacious lobby was fragrant with flowers and the check-in smooth.

Trent had arranged the accommodations and I had no need to pinch pennies. I usually traveled on local transport, staying in rooms where, if I was lucky, there was a ceiling fan to move the air and a mosquito net that had no holes. Living at street level has its advantages, especially if you can pick up some of the language. Still, I could enjoy luxury when I was not paying.

My room on the twenty-first floor of the Grand China Princess was spacious and airy. A card of welcome on the pillow sitting next to a bright yellow flower. The porter put my bags in the closet, showed me the safe, the complimentary robe and slippers. When he left, I grabbed a Heineken out of the bar fridge, slid open the glass door and stepped out onto the balcony. Sudden transition from air conditioning to that wonderful, warm, enveloping night air that pervades tropical latitudes.

"Take some time to get your bearings," Trent had said, "get over your jet lag. Hotel's on me. I get a deal because I stay there whenever I'm in good old Krung Thep." Krung Thep, city of angels, is what the Thais call Bangkok.

So for the next few days I did the tourist thing, visited the Grand Palace and my old haunts near Chao San Road. The pedestrian street still looked much the same as it had twenty years ago, full of Farang backpackers, bars, tattoo parlors, and stalls selling everything from counterfeit designer luggage to pirated CD's and DVD's. When I reached the end of the road, I crossed to the *wat* I remembered from my last stay. Trent and I had regarded this temple as our local *wat* and walked through it most days. I loved the Brahma bulls that just wandered around the grounds. We would sit on the steps of the temple, soothed by the hypnotic chanting. Sometimes the *wat* would be filled with the sounds of children being fed and instructed by the monks. Outside, carefully lined up, would be a row of tiny flip-flops.

"We could become monks," Trent had said one day.

I had laughed. "Us?"

"Sure. Most Thai men join a monastery at some point. They don't ask you to commit forever. You can stay a week, a month, even a lifetime."

"Become a *bikkhu*? Not for me," I had told him. "You can't eat after noon. And you have to get up before dawn."

"You might surprise yourself and like it."

"Not a chance. Don't forget, I gave up wearing a monk's habit at around five."

Trent laughed. "Never say 'never.'"

The *wat* had doubled in size since my last visit but still it was an oasis of quiet after the bustle of Bangkok street life. I wandered through the grounds and came across an old, white Mercedes on blocks serving as a chicken coop. The monks had a sense of humour. As I emerged into the quiet, leafy street behind the *wat*, the deep-throated bell sounded in a slow rhythm.

For some time I stood there looking up at the white bell tower, surprised at a sudden rush of emotion. Now that I had reached fifty-one the idea of becoming a monk, at least for a time, no longer felt totally out of the question. Maybe after I had lived here for a few years, I might find myself trying the life of a Fra Farang, but only for a month or so. Good karma.

For the four days of my stay, I rode tuk tuks and river buses around to see the sights, tried the new skytrain and avoided the giant Asian malls. No other city combines the sacred and the sensual the way Bangkok does, so by day I visited the Grand Palace, the Emerald Buddha, the Temple of the Dawn but by night I was drawn to the pleasures of Pat Pong and Soi Cowboy.

When I checked out, I took one of the pink Bangkok taxis to the bus depot. Trent had arranged for a car and driver but I figured I would save money canceling the driver, taking the local bus and pocketing the difference. I was not short of money but I guess old habits die hard and besides I always got a better feel for a place traveling at street level. Trent had emailed me that he had booked a room at a hotel on Bus Station *Soi* in Cha am so I should arrive in the right area.

The blue bus from Bangkok pulled in about two-thirty and parked at the top of Bus Station Soi. The highway had been four lane all the way because the royal family has a place in Hua Hin, just a few klicks south of Cha am. The only time the traffic slowed down was for a police check where the cops were flagging down all the heavy transports heading south and charging them 500 baht each for being "overloaded". Thai cops making a living.

When I got off, I found myself only a few steps from O'Doul's, Trent's Irish Pub. In the heat of the day, the pub was empty except for a couple of Thai waitresses and a middle-aged Farang, his beer belly pushing out a garish Hawaiian shirt. He turned out to be Jack, Trent's Aussie manager, who confirmed that Trent would be back around eight, or nine. I spent a pleasant hour there drinking ice-cold Singha beer and flirting with the two Thai girls who were serving. "He's got you a room on Whore Street," Jack told me.

"I thought I was staying on Bus Station Soi," I told him.

"Same thing. Everybody calls it Whore Street round here."

"He hasn't booked me into a 'short time' has he?"

"No, no. Charlie's place is a regular hotel. Mind you, he does rent out the washroom on the ground floor to the hookers from the street bars. Trent booked you into Charlie's My House Hotel while the races were on. Charlie was about the only one with rooms. Races just finished though so if you don't like Charlie's you can find something else. All the buses are headed back to Bangkok. I'll take you round if you like."

"No. I'll be fine. I guess I'll get over there, dispose of my luggage, have a look around."

"Sure. Beach is just down the bottom of the street. Can't miss it."

Not surprisingly, Whore Street was all but deserted in the afternoon heat. The strip of bars that occupied the middle of the road were all shuttered at that time of day. Halfway down the gently sloping street, I found Charlie's place, Cha am My House Hotel. I stepped into the shade of the open lobby and waited for someone to appear. A chubby middle-aged woman emerged from a back room frowning and stifling a yawn. I must have interrupted her afternoon siesta.

"You room second floor," she said, handing me a key attached to a large wooden elephant. As I walked the few steps to the elevator, I noticed that there was a full public washroom just past the reception desk and remembered that the whores used it at night. The elevator creaked and bumped alarmingly but made it to the next floor. My room was passable and, when I turned it on, the air conditioner worked, but noisily. I went into the bathroom to piss out some of the beer I had downed at O'Doul's. The light was a dim florescent tube over the sink which gave my face a green cast. I looked around. In the corner of the shower was a plastic shower cap over a large pipe. That explained the note on the wall:

> *Water bag is for hold down the sewer's smell*
> *Please removing when taking shower*
> *thank you*
> *Cha am my house Hotel*

No flower on the pillow either.

I dumped my luggage, crossed to the patio doors and stepped out on to the tiny balcony. The street below was still deserted but since I did not want to pass the next few hours watching Thai television, I took the stairs down to the lobby.

"Ah, welcome to My House," said a man with an unusually large square head and a ready smile. "I am Charlie."

I told him my name and we shook hands. "Pretty quiet here," I added by way of small talk.

"Oh yes. Last day of the jet ski races. Many leaving already. Very quiet." He paused. "You friend of Trent, huh?"

"Yeah."

"You know Trent long?"

"For a while," I said and handed him my room key. "I guess I'll wander around, see the town."

I walked down Bus Station Soi until I reached the beach road. There a succession of buses painted in wild colours began to pass me. All were playing Thai music at high volume and heading back to Bangkok.

As I crossed the road and walked under the beach trees, the sky opened up and I found a spot under a vacant beach umbrella. Soon even the horses had taken shelter under a plastic tarpaulin that was rapidly filling with water. I wouldn't have thought that they would mind the rain. The elephant, on the other hand, stood stoically in the downpour that was pelting the umbrellas, pock-marking the surf and carpet bombing the sand on the beach. Was he enjoying the cooling rain or did he know that there was no shelter here for such a creature? Hard to tell with an elephant. His mahout had tucked the elephant's bag of sugarcane under his arm and retreated under the nearest umbrella.

Other than the elephant, the beach was all but deserted. The Thai families and the beach sellers were crowded under the long lines of umbrellas nestled under the beach trees, talking, laughing, and breaking out food for picnics. A few of the braver kids ran out laughing into the warm rain pursued by the panicked cries of their elders. One boy even ventured into the surf only to be swept up by one of the beach sellers and carried back to his parents.

Cha am, two hours south of Bangkok, caters almost exclusively to Thai vacationers. Most of the Farangs come no closer than Hua Hin, an upmarket beach town to the south where the king himself has a residence. My friend, Trent, claimed that you could see Hua Hin from here when the weather was clear, its highrise hotels looming up on the distant curve of the bay.

One of the blue plastic tarps suddenly gave way, soaking an entire family and provoking squeals and gales of good-natured laughter from those around them. The rain stopped as suddenly as it had begun and soon the late afternoon sun was filtering through the lacy leaves of the trees. In another hour it would set over the mountains beyond the town. Idly, I walked along the beach, the only Farang in sight. Already sellers were back on the beach offering their wares. A boy began to fly a small plastic kite shaped like a biplane complete with spinning propeller. He smiled at me and offered me one for fifty baht. I shook my head and walked on. Jack had said that Trent might not be back before nine so I had some time to kill.

When darkness fell, I retreated to a small bar at the bottom of Whore Street and found a seat facing the beach road. I ordered a Chang beer and watched the people passing. A woman approached riding a bicycle cart and pulled it off the road on the beach side. There she turned on a florescent light and began to arrange the food and cooking utensils. The first of the night stalls.

When I had finished my beer and paid the Farang who ran the place with his Thai wife, I wandered back down the beach road. The beach side which had been almost empty in the late afternoon was now lined with night stalls selling food and drink. The symphony of smells was tantalizing as I passed stall after stall selling shrimps, fish, pork, chicken and even cakes and candies that only appear after dark because they would melt in the heat of the day. Finally I stopped at a stall and, by pointing, I managed to order some sticky rice smothered in pork marinated in soy sauce. At the next stall I picked up a Coke and wandered down to the beach to eat supper, wondering what the temperature was back home in Northern Ontario.

When I had finished I walked back to Bus Station Soi. The wide street had been transformed by a profusion of multicoloured lights sparkling from neon signs and spilling out of the bars that occupied the middle of the wide boulevard. Nowhere in the world, I think, is the difference between night and day so striking as in Thailand.

"Hallo! Where you from?" as I passed the bars at the bottom of the street. I waved at the beautiful, smiling girls and turned into the only bar with a pool table. It had been years since I had played but I used to be pretty good. This early the table was empty so I motioned to one of the taller bar girls that I wanted to play. She smiled, eyed me up and down and said in good English, "I think you will need a long one." I laughed and caught a reflection of my self in the mirror over the bar. Yeah, I am tall but that's not what she was talking about. I still had a full head of hair, dyed to my original dark brown, diamond stud in the right ear from Samantha, ears too big to be cute, but I was in pretty good shape for fifty-one. And retired now. Freedom fifty-one had been looking good so far. I was still healthy and so were my investments. Greg Paulsen was getting me a return of 9.6% in the market. For the first time ever, I had made enough money that I could afford most things. As some schmuck in the movies always said, "What could possibly go wrong?"

"You want somebody to play with?" she asked as she handed me the cue.

"Pool? Sure," I told her. "Maybe play different games later."

She nodded, leaned in so close that I could feel her soft breath in my ear and whispered, "My bar fine is only one hundred bhat."

"Pool first. You break."

She grabbed a cue from the end of the rack and hammered the cue ball so that one of the striped balls dropped into a corner pocket. She followed by potting three more balls before missing and turning the table over to me. "You've played a lot," I said, startled by the fact that she was not going to just let me win.

Gesturing around the tiny bar, she said, "Not much else to do here."

She won that first game and the next. Maybe she let up after that because I squeaked a win in the third game.

"You're a good player," she said as I finished my beer. Taking the empty bottle from me she set it down on a table, put one arm around me and her other hand gently on my crotch. Her breath held a slight tang of lime as she leaned into me. "One hundred baht."

"For the game?"

"For bar fine."

I paid the bar fine and the drinks tab and then she took my arm and led the way across the street. " What's your name?" I asked. "I'm Dan."

"Fon," she said. With that, she put my arm around her shoulder and lowered her head as if she did not want to be recognized. I looked around but all I could see were a couple of bar girls and a Farang watching us from the Butterfly Bar fifty metres up the street. Briefly I wondered if the other Farang might prove to be trouble but then Fon reached up and kissed me as we got to the door and I decided not to worry about it.

Closing the door behind us, she led the way upstairs to a tiny studio apartment. "Nice place Fon," I said as she turned on a single low wattage bedside lamp that gave a cozy glow to the place. On one side of the room, a tiny kitchen area with a counter and a couple of stools; on the other, the large bed with mirror tiles on the ceiling. No TV that I could see. The place was spotless.

"I own it," she told me.

"Oh," was my lame response. I watched as she went over to a small altar jutting out from the wall. She lit a couple of candles and three joss sticks, performed a wai and turned back to me, smiling.

"I own the little bar with the pool table too."

"If you own the place, why did I have to pay the bar fine?"
No flies on me.

She laughed and, with a single practiced gesture, pulled off
her top. Small breasts, of course, but perfectly formed. "The bartender, he works for me. Did you not expect to pay a bar fine?"

"Yes, but…"

"Then so far, I have not disappointed your expectations."

My turn to laugh. She nodded, then without a word began
to undress me. I watched her face, a slight smile. I guessed her
age at around twenty-four. One thing for sure, she had not just
arrived from the hill villages in the north.

When we were both naked, I reached for her but she
stepped back and said, "Shower first."

"Okay."

"And no sex without a condom."

"Wouldn't dream of it."

In the shower, she instructed me to just relax while she gave
me a combination shower/massage that made me somehow
horny and relaxed at the same time. After she dried me off,
she led me to the bed and pulled out a bottle of Mekong and
two glasses. "To us," she toasted.

"To us."

What can I tell you? The sex was amazing. When I paid
her, she got up, put on a silk robe and lit a cigarette. "You are
incredible, Fon," I told her.

We shared another glass of Mekong whisky. "To us," I said
again. "May there be many more nights just like this one."

When she replied, "I think there might be, Logan," I nearly
choked on the whisky. How the hell had she known my real
name? When I had recovered, I said, "What's your real name?"

"Fon."

"I always use a false name when I'm…"

"Yes, of course, but this is not Bangkok. Cha am is a small place. Not many Farangs live here. By now everyone knows there is a new Farang in town. Jack told me about you this afternoon."

We talked for a while, then made love again, slower this time, and then she said, "I have to go."

"Sure, but let's do this again," I said as I handed her a wad of Thai baht that she palmed expertly.

She kissed me and whispered, "Later tonight. No bar fine this time."

At the door to the street she peered out. "Wait here five minutes before you leave. When you see me later, act as if we are meeting for the first time."

"Sure." But my instincts were already telling me that I had made some kind of mistake that could cost me big time. The Farang that was staring at us as we crossed the road? I felt in my pocket for the sailor's knife I usually carry in case of trouble. It contained a razor-sharp blade and a marlin spike of hardened steel.

But after the jet ski races the street was all but empty. As I walked up the hill towards O'Doul's, a chorus of "Hello. Welcome," from the girls in the bars I passed. Scared of your own shadow, I told myself.

Even before I turned the corner at the top of Whore Street, I could hear the music coming from O'Doul's. Light was streaming though the open gates of the patio. On top of the wall that masks the patio on the street side were six cheap, painted statues of women holding up lighted torches, the wires, as usual, clearly visible. The sandwich board outside was also lit and proclaimed, "Under New Management."

Still wondering about Fon's insistence that we pretend we'd never met, I edged cautiously down the other side of the road until I reached a black Mercedes parked across from the gate to O'Doul's. The car had not been there this afternoon so I suspected it belonged to Trent. Probably a rental since he lived in Australia most of the time.

Through the gate, I could see that several of the tables were occupied by Farangs, even some children. A few people were dancing. To my left, beyond the tables, was a couch near the short flight of steps that led up into the air-conditioned dining room. Jack was sitting there with his arm around Fon. Shit! So that's what her little song-and-dance was about. Nothing to do but tough it out.

I paused just inside the gate and looked around. To my right, a small stage where two musicians were performing songs in English. Above them was the omnipresent spirit house. While I watched one of the Thai waitresses stood on a chair and put some red blossoms in front of it, with a glass of what looked like Mekong whiskey. Then she lit two candles. From somewhere in my memory, I pulled up the saying, "Blossoms for beauty, medicine for health, candles for enlightenment." The waitress made a wai, got down and went back to serving the customers.

"He's here, Trent! Your mate," Jack yelled into the small room behind the bar. "How ya goin'?" I turned. Jack was smiling at me, even clapped me on the back. The greeting seemed genuine so I guessed that he did not know.

"Me, I'm terrific," I told him. "Looks like your doing pretty good business."

"Always do on the weekends when Larry and Susan are playing. Most of the people at the tables are Scandies." Scandies? A lot of blondes in the crowd. Oh, right, Scandinavians. "Watcha drinking?"

"Bottle of Singha beer."

Jack nodded to one of the Thai waitresses who smiled at me and headed towards the bar. Jack put his arm around me and led me through the dancers to the couch. "Logan, I'd like you to meet my girl friend, Fon. Fon this is Trent's friend from Canada."

Fon rose and shook my hand. "Pleased to meet you. How was your trip?"

"Long, but I stayed over in Sydney for a few days, actually in Manly Beach, and then flew on to Bangkok."

"Another nine sodding hours in the air," said Jack. "Have to take that flight every time I renew the bloody visa." My beer arrived as we were sitting down.

"Right," I said, taking a pull at my bottle. Glancing at Fon, I caught her looking at me with an ironic smile. Didn't take a genius to figure this woman could be dangerous for my health.

"Cheers mate! Welcome to the land of lust," Jack toasted, and we all clinked our glasses.

Larry and Susan finished "Dancing Queen" and Larry said into the mike, "Back in a few minutes."

"While we're taking a break," added Susan, "think of any favourites you'd like us to play." They left the stage to a smattering of applause.

"They're Philippinos," said Jack. "Took a lot of haggling to get them down to a price we could afford, but they do bring in the customers."

"I thought Cha am was strictly a Thai resort."

"It is but there's some new holiday condos up the Beach Road towards Hua Hin. S'full of Scandies. Course, there's always the ex-pats. That's them around the bar watching footie."

I looked over. Three middle-aged white guys were propped up on the bar stools watching Aussie rules football playing soundlessly on a wide screen TV.

"I'll introduce you if you like," said Jack.

"Okay," I said, not trusting myself or Fon to carry on any more small talk with Jack.

"Hey, you arseholes, meet our newest ex-pat. Name's Logan. All the way from the wilds of Canada." He patted me on the shoulder. "I'll leave you in their capable hands. Better get back to work."

"Sure."

"Canada. Never got up there. I'm from New York. Billy. Good to meet you." The accent sounded authentic.

"Good to meet you, Billy."

"This here's Ken from Australia," he said, pointing at the morose fat man perched improbably on a stool at the end of the U-shaped bar.

"And I'm Sean," offered the middle-aged Irishman with an impressive belly.

"I'm glad to find at least one Irishman in an Irish pub," I told him.

"Can't let the best Irish bar south of Bangkok limp along without a real son of Erin. And this is Chimlin, my assistant." Out of the corner of my eye, I saw an ironic smirk crease Billy's face. Catching my eye, he lifted his eyebrows in mock disbelief.

"*Sawadee*, Chimlin," I say.

Chimlin nodded and smiled and I wondered if this *katoey*, this Thai she/male, spoke English. She was expertly made up

and the adam's apple was not obvious. With a languid movement, she patted her hair. The large hands, although carefully
manicured, gave him away. Chimlin noticed me watching and
put his hand into Sean's lap, flashing me a sad smile.

"Trent said he had a buddy coming down from Canada."
Billy. For the first time in the low light, I got a good look at him:
a middle-aged New Yorker with small, dark eyes, a sallow com-
plexion, dyed black hair, thinning on top and ending in a scrag-
gly ponytail. He was wearing the ex-pat uniform: faded ⊤, shorts
and flip-flops. "Says you're planning to stay on in Cha am."

"I'm going to give it a shot."

The ex-pats sniffed around me, the new dog trying to join
the pack. Over the next couple of hours, I bought a couple of
rounds and listened to the bragging and bullshit. Billy turned
out to be the leader of the pack. When he told me he knew of
a place to stay if I was interested, I readily agreed. We arranged
to meet the next day.

During the inevitable lulls in the conversation, I got a closer
look at Trent's new place. The only indications that O'Doul's
was an Irish pub were an old Guinness poster showing the
pubs of Dublin, a scruffy poster full of Irish writers, a couple
of supporter's scarves and a hurley stick arranged over the
television.

For a while I watched Larry and Susan play and a very
Siamese cat, with the odd twisted tail they have here, leap lightly
on to the altar, and then sip the whiskey with obvious relish.

"Noi always puts the best whiskey out for the cat." A voice
behind me. "Sorry I took so long. It's tax time. Had to get it
done."

"Great to see you, Trent."

"You too, mate." A quick hug. "Been a while."

"Nearly three years since opal hunting in Coober Pedy."

Trent laughed. "Bastards must have seen us coming. Professional red dirt salesmen."

"And the heat! Unbelievable!"

"Sure. No wonder everybody there lives underground."

A pause while Trent ordered drinks and then, "Cheers, mate! To one day finding the mother lode."

Old times. But why had he waited two hours before coming out of his air-conditioned office to see me?

"Still, you must be doing all right, chucking it all in and coming to live in the Land of Smiles."

"Sold the marina. Friend of mine is investing the money for me. Greg Paulsen. Remember him?"

"Vaguely. Wasn't he up on some insider trading charge?"

"They dropped it. Anyway, he's opened an investment consultancy business, only lets close friends in. After the charge he's paranoid about dealing with the wrong people. Anyway, he's got us in off shore investments that are returning anything from nine to fourteen percent."

"Sounds too good to be true."

Trent's superior tone irritated me. "Don't think I didn't check him out. He's even got his own family in his investment group. I doubt he'd rob his own grandmother."

"Hey, no need to jump all over me," Trent said, holding up his hands in mock surrender. "I'm just pleased you made it."

"No worries. But you never told me"—I took a sip of my beer, then continued, with more edge than I had intended—"how you managed to buy O'Doul's. I thought you had to have a Thai partner who owned at least 51%."

He leaned over so no one else could hear him. "I bought the place from John O'Doul. John's wife, Barbara, controls all his finances. She's got some kind of special Thai status. Don't know who she pays off but…Anyway, she's the silent partner."

"Clever deal," I said and meant it. Most Farangs simply married a Thai woman and her name appeared as the majority owner.

"Yeah. Makes more sense to me than getting married again," he said with a mock shudder.

I nodded. Trent had sworn off women. Wouldn't even look at the Thai whores. Blamed it on his three marriages: the French Canadian artist who cracked him over the head with a wine bottle, no word on the vintage, the Canadian nurse who supported him while his software business in Sudbury was gradually going under, and the anorexic blonde who slept with the best man at their Caribbean wedding.

"Let's move over to a table," Trent suggested.

"Sure." As good a way to change the subject as any. We found a table near the fountain, away from the band. My lead: "Billy's gonna show me a place tomorrow."

"Billy?" Trent nodded. "Either he owns the place or is getting a kickback. Billy doesn't do anything for nothing."

"I'll keep my eyes open." I looked over at the bar. Billy was looking at us but turned away and said something to Ken when I caught his eye.

"Get Fon to go with you. Have you met Fon yet? Jack's girlfriend?"

Now's not the time, I cautioned myself. "Sure, Jack introduced us. I'll ask her later."

"Great! How's your room?"

"Oh, fine. Charlie seems okay."

"Yeah, it's his wife you have to worry about."

"How about you? Still sworn off women."

"Oh, yeah. Easier than I thought." He laughed and slapped me on the shoulder. "We'll have to get down south to Krabi, and Phuket. You'll be amazed at how much it's changed."

We talked for twenty minutes or so before Larry and Susan ended their break, then Trent got up. "Back to the salt mines."

"Sure. I'll grab something to eat."

"I'll send Noi over with a menu. Food's good here. Try the soup, chicken and coriander. Prayon is a great cook. John O'Doul was over to teach him how to make Irish stew last week."

"I'll try the soup."

"Good. Oh, and you're money's no good here. Okay?"

"Okay, and thanks."

"No worries."

I settled for the soup and the sea bass in sweet chilli sauce. The food was terrific. Just as I was finishing up, Fon came over. I looked around and located Jack sitting at the bar with the ex-pats. His back was to me.

"I told Jack I am going home early. See you at my bar." Before I could say anything she moved off. A trace of her perfume hung in the air.

I watched her as she chatted with a family of blonde Scandies. She was a good looking woman but I would be crazy not to give her bar a wide berth. And the longer I sat and mulled the situation over, the more tempted I was. After all if Jack found out that I'd done his girlfriend he was not going to believe I didn't know who she was. On the other hand, I could have an early night.

I risked a glance. She was kissing Jack goodbye. He patted her ass as she left. As she passed me on her way out, she whispered, "Twenty minutes."

Half an hour later, I finished my beer and wandered over to the ex-pats. "Think I'll have an early night," I said to Jack. And to Billy, "See you tomorrow about ten?"

"Yeah. Why don't we meet at Neise's and have breakfast."

"Sure. Where's that?"

He explained that it was north just off the beach road. "Look for the internet café and turn left. It's only a few yards up the road."

Turning away from the others, Jack gave me a theatrical wink. "Don't worry about the bill. I'll put it on your tab."

"Good to meet you," I said.

"Any friend of Trent's, you know..."

"Yeah. Where is he?"

"Oh, he's back fiddling the books."

"Tell him I'll see him tomorrow afternoon. May even have a place by then."

"No worries."

Whore Street was not very noisy. Sure, all the bars played music but not at earsplitting volume. Christ, I thought, I must be getting old. I used to like that kind of excitement. As I reached the Butterfly Bar, three up from Fon's place, I hesitated, still not decided about taking a chance with Fon again.

"Hello, welcome."

I turned and saw a tiny, beautiful woman wearing a tight T, a wraparound skirt and over-the-knee black boots. "*Sawadee*," I said and offered her my imitation of a wai.

She smiled. "Where you from?"

"Canada."

"You like buy me a drink?"

I thought of Fon, waiting a couple of bars down. "Yeah, why not?" I was growing to like Jack and now that I knew about his relationship with Fon, dumb though it was, I did not want to carry on with her, no matter how attractive she was. "What'll it be? My name is, ah, Logan." No sense lying.

"Champagne cocktail," she replied as I slid onto the bar stool beside her.

I ordered a beer and whatever concoction passed for a champagne cocktail here. The sound system was playing Tom Cochrane's "Life is a Highway."

"I'm not the only Canadian here tonight," I said, pointing to the speakers. "The guy singing this song is Canadian too."

"Ah, yes," she said and, right then, I realized that she did not speak much English. If I was going to stay here, I was going to have to learn some serious Thai. She ran her hand lightly up my leg. In the low red/amber lights flickering to the music, she looked absolutely beautiful as we drank to nothing in particular.

"What should I call you?"

"G.I. Jane." Okay.

Then down to business. "What's the bar fine?"

She told me and then asked, "You have room?"

"Yeah. At My Hotel." I pointed across the street.

She laughed, "Ah, Charlie's. I use water room there."

"Washroom?"

"Washroom, yes." Right. The one off the lobby.

This time I remembered to negotiate and ended up paying her for "long time." Nice to sleep with somebody through the night. I had not done so for quite a while. Don't forget to hide money and passport, I reminded myself as we crossed the road. I hoped Fon was not watching but didn't risk looking back.

Charlie's wife was watching television. When she saw me

with G.I. Jane she scowled and said something that even I could tell was rude. Both erupted in rapid fire Thai.

"Hey!" I said loudly to get the floor. Both women stopped and stared at me. I shoved two hundred baht into Mrs. Charlie's hand. She nodded, tossed my key on the counter will ill grace and went back to the television.

G.I. Jane hugged me as we went up the stairs. The sight, the smell of her, together with the little war downstairs had me so horny that I had barely closed the door before we had sex against the wall, me holding her in midair by her ass, the leather boots flailing at my thighs. She chuckled and buried her tongue in my mouth.

G.I. Jane stayed the night and I found I enjoyed sleeping with her as much as the sex. I had suffered from insomnia for what seemed like forever but beside Jane I managed to drift off fairly quickly. Every once in a while I awoke and looked at her sleeping curled up beside me, sometimes with her head on my chest. I found myself stroking her thick black hair, smiling contentedly into the semi-darkness and listening to the music of the street.

Next morning I made my way down the beach road, turned up past a Thai restaurant catering only to locals. Food looked good. Next door was Neise's advertising a full Aussie breakfast for only 99 baht.

Billy was not there when I arrived at precisely ten. Of course, Thai time I told myself and grabbed the well-read copy of the *Bangkok Post*. On the front page was a picture of a small Thai child wearing a surgical mask. The caption read, "The Mask of Horror." The story underneath warned that the swine flu pandemic would kill millions around the world. I had noticed some people, mostly women, wearing masks in Bangkok but only one woman so far, a vegetable seller, in Cha am.

"Hey, you not allowed in here no more." I looked up to see a middle-aged Thai woman berating an old, balding ex-pat.

"I'm just here to see my friend."

"You no pay. You not welcome here."

"She's right." This from a tall gaunt Australian who I guessed nominally owned the restaurant that was in his wife's name.

"Bloody woman can't cook a decent egg to save her life," the old ex-pat muttered as he beat a strategic retreat.

Two of the other tables were occupied by solitary Farangs eating hearty western breakfasts. The Thai woman turned up and handed me a menu. "What you like?"

"Coffee, the Aussie breakfast and an orange juice if you have one."

"We have only lemonade and pineapple juice," she said. "Sorry."

"Lemonade then, but coffee first."

I passed the time doing the crossword in the *Post* and watching a small Thai boy climbing on a large Harley motorcycle parked on the side of the patio. Quite a few locals in the Thai restaurant next door, clearly visible beyond a low brick wall, but it might as well have been in a different universe.

Billy turned up at the same time as my breakfast and ordered a Heineken. "Can't stand the Thai stuff," he told me. "Rumour is they put formaldehyde in the Singha."

I had heard the same rumour twenty years ago so just nodded as I tried the sausages.

"Good breakfast," I told him. "You having some?"

"Nah. My ol' lady already got me breakfast. She's a great cook."

"You married?"

"Not so as you'd notice." He took a long pull at his beer, then lit a cigarette. "In a way, I had to get married."

"Old man have a shotgun?"

He laughed. "No, no. Sammy can't have kids. I had to marry her because Farangs can't really own property here. To get a bar, I had to put it in the name of a Thai. Well, I trusted her better than anybody else."

"How long you been married?"

"What? Oh, year, year and a half. You know how it is. Men were never meant to be...ah, what's the word...monogamous, so I get to sample all the time. She doesn't mind. Thai women... worse you treat them, better they like it. I swear to God!"

Yeah, Billy was a charmer all right. "Where is your bar?"

"Well, it's not open yet. Still doing some renos."

I finished my coffee. "So, did you find me a place?"

"I got a couple in mind. Depends on how much you're willing to pay, how much space you want, all that crap."

"Well, I'm hoping that I'll be sharing it with someone else eventually so something not too small. I got a little money put by. Made some good investments."

"Hey, Neville!" shouted Billy. The Aussie proprietor sauntered over. "Meet my friend, Logan. Fresh blood. He's looking for a place. Know of something that'll suit him?"

"G'day, mate," said Neville. "Welcome to Cha am. I noticed a listing on the bulletin board at the cyber café. It's a bungalow, inland a couple of streets near the indoor market. It's a furnished house but going at a good price."

"Sounds good."

"Course, if you want a place on the beach road..."

"No, no. A couple of blocks up would be ideal," I said.

"We'll find you something great," said Billy. "Oh, wasn't Fon coming to translate?"

"Yeah, I guess she forgot."

Billy cocks one eyebrow and looks at me askance. "You didn't!"

"Didn't what?"

"You fucked her."

"No, no. Well, yeah, but that was before I knew she was Jack's."

Billy put his arm around me. "Don't worry about it. Fon's still on the game. Only person doesn't know…no, doesn't *want* to know, is Jack. He thinks he's going to marry the bitch."

"Will he find out?"

"Ah, somebody'll tell him but he won't believe it. If he asks, just tell him you don't know what he's talking about. Hell, I've had her more'n enough times."

As I was paying for breakfast and Billy's beer, Neville suddenly rushed over and picked up the boy who was playing on the motorcycle, scolding him in halting Thai as I was pocketing the change. The boy ran and sheltered behind my leg, peaking out at Neville. Neville smiled and shook his head. "He knows he's not supposed to touch the bike."

The boy looked up at me, his eyes big. "Don't worry," I told him. "I won't turn you in."

He gave me a big grin and ran back to the kitchen to find his mother. "He's got good taste," Billy told Neville. "That Fatboy is a sweet machine. Don't forget, if you ever decide to sell, call me first."

Billy and I dropped into the cyber café on the corner to check out the bulletin board. "You're all right, Logan," Billy told me, "for a Canuck. Don't worry. We'll get you a sweet place."

Give him his due, Billy spent a lot of time ferrying me around in his old Nissan to look at places over the next few days and I finally picked a beautiful nearly-new bungalow just a block up from the beach. After a half day of bartering, I got the place for less that three million baht, about a hundred and ten grand Canadian after all the fees and ancillaries. With Trent's help, I hired a maid/cook and a gardener and I was set, sure I had made the right choice. The future was so bright I had to wear shades.

I was even developing a routine. Most days it was Neise's for breakfast, then I checked my email at the cyber café and wandered down to the beach where I rented a deck chair under the trees. For a couple of hours I swam in the warm surf and read or listened to tunes on my iPod. Occasionally I rented a horse and rode full gallop on the wet sand. Some lunch from the beach stalls, back home for a siesta, dinner and drinks at O'Doul's with the other ex-pats.

Most were married to Thai women but the wives almost never turned up with them. Instead the guys hung around the bar. The list of topics was short: local gossip about whatever ex-pats were not there, sports with obscure rules like Aussie Rules Football and cricket, wild fantasies about sexual prowess, the poor state of Thai stick and the laziness of the Thais. Yeah, I could see why they were here. Where else could these middle-aged, out-of-shape guys live so well for so little? Except for Trent and Jack, and the two Irishmen, John, the original owner of the bar, and Sean with his boy toy, they were tiresome assholes to a man. But then who else was there I could talk to? Very few of the locals were fluent in English.

On the plus side, most of the ex-pats would have your back if need be. Still, if I was going to live here, I needed to learn Thai. I don't have a bad ear so I was picking up the usual conversational stuff but when I looked at the written script with no gaps to signal where one word ended and the next began, I just put the decision off for another day or two.

Don't get me wrong, some nights the ex-pats were entertaining, their stories funny. After smoking a little stick and downing a few beers, I appreciated their camaraderie and decided that they were not such a bad bunch after all. There were times when Prayon cooked me yet another great meal and even took me into the kitchen to see how it was made, times when I looked around at the Scandie tourists enjoying themselves, times when Larry and Susan performed an oldie that brought a lump to my throat, times when John narrated one of his tall tales about the days he played International Rugby for the Irish, times when I puffed with pride at the mere thought of actually owning a house here, times when I knew that I had found paradise on the shores of the Gulf of Siam.

And there was always Whore Street. A couple of weeks after my arrival in Cha am, I left O'Doul's sometime around one. Most of the Scandies had departed for their condos by midnight and I ended the evening sitting on the couch talking to Trent and Jack. Fon was stroking Jack and he seemed to be enjoying the feeling. Occasionally she glanced at me and flashed a wicked little smile. I had stayed clear of her since I found out that Jack was crazy about her. But when she knew Jack was not looking, she still gave me that look. Tonight, I had had enough so I made my apologies and left.

I dropped into the Butterfly Bar for a nightcap, or at least that is what I told myself. G.I. Jane was not there, but after less than a minute an absolutely stunning girl came over. She was wearing leather pants and high heels despite the heat. She told me her name was Malee, which means jasmine. Malee's English was a lot better than Jane's.

We spent the night in my room at Charlie's place. She told me about her family in a tiny village up north near the border with Laos, about how hard it was for farmers to make a living. I found her easy to talk to, even found myself opening up to her about my life back in the great white north. I told her I had picked up a degree in philosophy and English from University of Toronto, about the various jobs I had held and about my last business venture, the marina on Lake Wanapitae near Sudbury. In the summers, I rented out my 28 slips to boaters and charged the weekend crowd to launch at my ramp. In the winter, I rented out huts for ice fishing.

"Ice fishing?"

I tried to explain but it is almost impossible for someone who has only seen ice in cubes to visualize ice stretching out to the horizon and beyond. In the end, I gave up and told her that running the marina was an ideal profession for an arts grad. "Lots of time to read and play my bass in the fall and in the spring I had time to travel. Her eyelids began to droop and I realized I was boring her so I turned the subject back to sex, a subject Malee had certainly mastered.

We spent the next six nights together. When she left that last morning, I reminded her that I was moving into my new house that day and that I was eager for her to see it. That night, though, she was not in the Butterfly Bar. Wanting to tell somebody, maybe to brag a little about my new place, I felt annoyed that she was missing. G.I. Jane was chatting up a customer and not looking my way, so I continued down the street and, what the hell, dropped into the Pool Bar. Fon was there.

She tossed a cue to me and said, "500 baht a game."

"Okay." Not that I had a chance of winning.

While we were playing, she asked, "Why did you go with G.I. Jane and then Malee? You a butterfly?"

"Butterfly?"

"A man who sleeps with lots of girls," she explained and added significantly, "a guy who cannot be trusted."

"Look, I didn't drop in the other night because I found out you were Jack's girlfriend. You might have warned me."

"I am not Jack's girl. He is just…" She shrugged, unable to find the word. "You know. He doesn't like to think I sleep with others. When I told him I needed money to send to my family, he offered to give me more, but I don't like to take advantage of him."

I conceded to myself that she had a point. Not her fault that love was blind, at least in Jack's case.

Fon let me win the second game so I only owed her 500 baht. I paid and she smiled as she tucked the notes away. "No bar fine this time," she told me.

And I was going to have an early night. Not the first time lust had beaten logic and, this being Thailand, likely not the last. Seemed a steep climb to the moral high ground and I was wearing the wrong shoes. Five minutes later she had talked to her bartender and we were leaving for her room.

Must have been close to three by the time we slipped out of her place. I decided to have one last drink with her before walking the few blocks to my new place. Suddenly a wild shriek tore out of the darkness and sent a shiver through me. Before I could even turn towards the sound, Malee hurtled out of the darkness yelling at Fon in Thai. Fon went down in a flurry of fists and hair-pulling. Jesus! In an instant, the gleam of a knife. The wild movement froze into a dangerous tableau as Fon held the knife to Malee's throat. Tears were running down Malee's face as more people arrived from the bars, drawn by the commotion. Gradually Malee swayed to her feet and backed away. I reached out towards her. Mistake. She bit my hand. "You big bastard, Farang!" she aimed at me, then she stumbled away up the street. I used my left hand to help Fon up.

"What was that about?" I asked her.

"Jealous," Fon explained, brushing herself off. "She thinks you should sleep with only her." She shrugged.

She assured everyone that she was all right but some of the whores were giving me hard stares as she led me across to Charlie's place to wash the blood off my hand.

An hour later, lying alone in bed, I went over the whole incident in my head. I could not sleep because my hand was throbbing. This being a butterfly was turning out to be bad for my health. Still, no woman had ever fought for me, certainly not with such fury. I was flattered. I thought of Malee for a long time, her beauty and her passion, and resolved to see her again, maybe even apologize.

Of course, by the time I got to Neise's for breakfast, everybody had heard about last night. "Hear you started a bitch fight," said Neville, laughing. I nodded and showed my bandaged hand. "The usual?"

"Sure." He brought over the *Bangkok Post*.

"Been saving it for you," he announced, tipped me a wink and wandered back to the kitchen.

Two Aussie ex-pats a couple of tables over gave me a thumbs-up and mumbled, "Good on ya, mate."

"Thanks," I said, and held up the bandaged hand, "but, as you can see, I lost."

"Ah, trick is to stay well clear when they get stuck in," one said confidently.

"I'll remember that for next time," I said and opened the paper to signal the end of the conversation only to find that the markets were dropping like a stone, something to do with subprime mortgages. Not a good sign, especially since I had spent a good chunk of my savings on the house. I had planned to spend the day looking for Malee to make things right between us, but now I decided that right after breakfast I needed to check my email at the cyber café on the corner.

Neville's wife brought me the Aussie breakfast and I began to eat, thinking about Greg and how well he had been handling my money. He would have foreseen this, I told myself. Guy is a genius with money. Still, all my eggs seemed to be in the same basket, an investment strategy that I suspected was not recommended by Warren Buffet.

By the time I pushed my plate away, Neise's was almost full of ex-pats, rare for this early, and there was a buzz of conversation. I caught snatches and realized that everyone was worried about the investments that let them live here.

"Okay if I sit here?" I looked up and saw Rex, an aging Vietnam vet.

"Help yourself," I said with more enthusiasm than I felt. I had had enough of his stories about killing charlie and, like everyone else, suspected that his heroic exploits were about as real as breast implants. But today, he was subdued.

"Just had a look at my investments," he said. "Don't look good."

"I'm just going to check myself," I told him, finishing the last of my coffee.

"Market has been tanking for three days now," he said. "I contacted my guy yesterday and told him to sell some stuff but he said, 'Don't. You'll just consolidate your losses.' So, against my better instincts, I let it ride. By the close of the market yesterday, my stocks were worth shit." His voice was hoarse. He was a good looking older guy, chiseled face, magnificent handlebar moustache, long full main of greying hair. I realized to my surprise I was beginning to feel sorry for him.

"Do you have any other money coming in?"

"Small vet pension."

"Hang in there, Rex," I said as I got up. "I'm just going to check on my finances. Wish me luck."

"Luck, man," he said, reaching out and shaking my hand with a heavy grip.

"Thanks."

When I got to the cyber café, all the computers were occupied by Farangs. I was the sixth person waiting. The crowd was overwhelming the air conditioning and there was an acrid smell of anxiety in the room.

"Let me know when my turn comes up," I told the Thai teenager manning the desk. "I'll be right outside."

Stepping over the yellow mutt sleeping on the step, I distracted myself by flipping through the rack of postcards. A middle-aged Farang came out, a stunned look on his face, and walked away slowly down the beach road in the direction of the fishing village. A nasty knot of worry began to form in my guts.

Another four ex-pats came out together, passed me and head down towards Whore Street.

"Still waiting?" I turned to see that Rex has returned to look disaster in the face again.

"Yeah, but I think it's about my turn. Wish me luck."

"Yeah."

The Thai boy never had any intention of calling me, of course, but there was a terminal open. I sat down, signed in, and started checking my email. Mostly spam from cut rate travel agencies, sheet music sites, marine suppliers and porn sites. No word from Greg. I fired off an email asking him how he was handling the crisis. While I was waiting, I checked Google News but it did not improve my mood. Panic selling, Fanny Mae going down, Goldman Sachs in trouble, armageddon. I called up the *New York Times* web page, same thing.

After a long five minutes, I got a reply that had obviously been sent to all Greg's investors assuring us that our money was safe but since he had it stashed offshore, he would not be ready to convert to cash until the markets stabilized. For our patience, he had issued a $1000 dividend to each investor regardless of the size of investment. So, did I believe him? Hey, benefit of the doubt. I sent off a reply thanking him for his prompt response. Sudbury had never seemed so far away.

Next I sent an email to my sister in Lively, a small town just outside Sudbury. I had talked her into investing with Greg and now I told her to hang in there, that Greg was a good guy. I did not say that if he wasn't, we were all going down with him.

Now I checked into my banking site. Sure enough there was an extra grand in my main account. The money for the bungalow and furnishings had come out already and the cash available was pretty depleted. For a minute, I stared at the screen, thinking about the $650,000 of my money in Greg's hands. Not broke yet, I comforted myself as I signed out. Hot in here though.

As I climb out of the chair, Rex, who had been waiting near the door, pushed forward to take my terminal. "How'd you make out?" he asked.

"Not broke yet," I told him, "worried though."

"You and me too, bro."

When I left, I bought a couple of ice-cold cokes, crossed the road and wandered down towards the water. Wind was pretty strong so the waves were curling in a little higher than usual. I hit the sand, kicked off my shoes and walked into the water. Not many people on the beach today. Walking in the surf I stopped and felt the receding wave suck the sand out from around my feet. When I was a kid, I used to get a scary thrill out of the feeling that the ground beneath my feet seemed to be opening up.

For an hour or two, I sat in the shade of the trees, trying to find an upside to the day. More than once, I thought of heading back to the cyber café and getting online again. Christ, Cha am seemed so far from anywhere. Yeah, well, that's why you chose it. Get your ass in gear, you've got a lady to locate.

The bars on Whore Street were closed at this hour so most of the afternoon I spent at O'Doul's. For a while I sat up at the bar where there was only one topic of conversation today: the great market dive. Trent had pulled up Australian Broadcasting on the TV's satellite feed. Whenever the news came on, we were all quietly glued to the screen. None of the financial news was good, no news of a turnaround, just the sounds of our money spiraling down the toilet.

Around four, I had a meal with Trent. He had lost maybe half a mill but he was still smiling. Why? Because when his Dad died he had inherited over 25 million Aussie dollars, much of it in precious metals, and they were doing way better than financials.

"How's your money?" he asked. I told him about Greg's email. "I guess every financial advisor in North America is sending out one of those."

"Hey, the guy knows what he's doing."

"Yeah, of course. It's just, well, you know, nobody knows where this is going. U.S. was a financial basket case even before this happened."

"Yeah," I conceded. "Can't say I'm not worried. Hey, got anything on for the next couple of hours?"

"What you got in mind?"

"A trip to Hua Hin."

"Sure, why not? I'll go wake up Jack."

"No hurry."

"He's been in there since noon, time he got his ass in gear."

On the way down to Hua Hin in Trent's Mercedes, we reminisced about Snow Where, the rock group we started back in the eighties when we were both living in Sudbury. Trent played rhythm guitar and sang leads while I played bass and sang harmonies. Tammy See was on drums and Nicky Polifroni played a mean lead guitar. We had played gigs all over the north, mostly on weekends, covering everything from Nirvana to the Stones with a few forgettable songs written by Nicky mixed in. After a couple of years it was not fun anymore; people started missing rehearsals so, just like a real band, we broke up.

"Whatever happened to Nicky?" Trent asked.

"Went to Toronto, tried to break into the big time. I think she ended up doing session work in Vancouver."

"Good for her."

A few minutes of silence while we watched the four-lane scudding by with its manicured median strip and huge pictures of the royal family spanning the highway. "Wonder what the king thinks when he comes down to his retreat," I said.

"Probably loves it. I would.... Any reason we're going to Hua Hin?" Like the rest of the ex-pats, Trent called the town 'Huey Hin' even though the Thai pronunciation was "Wha Heen." For my first few days here, I had thought they were two different places.

"I need to get a present for Malee," I told him.

Trent shook his head. "Don't make Jack's mistake."

"Malee's not like Fon."

"Well, you know my take on women. True love, especially in the Land of Smiles, is rare as rocking horse shit."

"Yeah, I know, I know. Remember Deb?" Deb and I had lived together for a miserable eighteen months.

"Jesus, she was a piece of work."

"Malee's not like that. I really think this is going to work."

"Okay. Not my business." Minutes later: "What you got in mind to get her?"

"Pendant, bracelet, something like that."

"I know just the place," he said, "but first Starbucks. I never come this way without getting a fix."

"Starbucks it is."

At Starbucks, if you did not look out the windows, and ignored the four Thai cops upstairs, you would swear you were in North America. The offerings were the same, same dumb sizes, same great coffee. "Ever think of going back?" Trent asked as I sipped my cappuccino grande.

"No, not a chance. Burnt too many bridges. Besides I sold the marina so there's nothing to go back to."

"It's different for me. Oz is only nine hours away and I have to go back every once in a while to renew my visa."

"Yeah."

Trent took me to a goldsmith and I picked out a gold chain with a small, oval-cut ruby pendant. Trent negotiated the price as he had some Thai and had dealt here before. Even though the chain and pendant were set into an elegant, blue velvet presentation box, the woman behind the counter insisted on wrapping it. The result, in red and gold paper, was charming.

"She's gonna love it," Trent said.

"I hope so. I haven't seen her since the fight with Fon last night."

"How's your hand, by the way?" He smirked.

"Don't remind me."

By the time we got back some of the bars had opened. I walked down to the Butterfly Bar and asked for Malee.

"She went up north." The bartender told me. To see her family, I assumed.

"Know when she's coming back?"

He just shrugged.

For the next four days I kept checking, but no news. On the afternoon of the fifth day the bartender at the Butterfly Bar smiles and says, "She back last night. Might be in later. You want drink?"

I fished in my pocket and handed him two one hundred baht notes. "You want to show me where she lives?"

He hesitated, but only for a second. "I can't leave right now." I went to put the money away.

"Wait." He called over one of the girls. After a rapid conversation in Thai he said, "She take you."

"Thanks," I said and began to turn away.

"Ah…"

Of course, the money. I handed it to him and left with the girl. She took me into some back alleys that I had never seen before. Eventually, she pointed to an unpainted door and nodded. "She here," she added for emphasis.

I knocked. When I looked around the girl had gone. No sound coming from inside. I tried the door. It was not locked and creaked as I pushed it back. Somewhere in the building, Thai pop music was playing. The room was dingy, four single mattresses on the floor, a dirty sink. A curtain hid the entrance to the rest of the house. And the smell, Jesus! No sign of Malee. Although I really wanted to leave, I forced myself to push through the curtain. A dark corridor with a worn staircase at the end. The first two rooms were empty. I found Malee seated on a mattress in the third one. Her few clothes were folded neatly at the end of her bed, her boots, shoes and rubber sandals in a box under the bedside lamp. On the other side of the tiny room sat a small altar with three josh sticks burning.

"What you come here for, Butterfly?" she asked, sulkily.

"You," I told her. "I've been looking for you but you were away."

"Yes. I went home. My father die."

"Sorry."

She shrugged but said nothing else. For a few seconds, I stood there wondering how to proceed. In the soft light, she was as beautiful as I had ever seen her. Finally, I knelt down beside her. "I really am sorry," I whispered. "No more butterfly. Only with Malee."

"No fucky-fucky with other girls?"

"No fucky-fucky. Only with Malee."

She looked me in the eye for the first time and gave me a smile that would break your heart. "Okay."

A fleeting thought, no more than a nanosecond, that maybe I was being conned; I dismissed it. "I think maybe I'm in love," I said on impulse.

Slowly, she began to undo my belt. "What's this?" she asked when she noticed the large bulge in my pocket.

"I'm happy to see you," I quipped but, of course, she missed the reference. "A present for Malee."

"What? What?"

I pulled out the beautiful package and put it on the box that held the lamp. "Later, I give. Now, we need to love," I told her.

She grabbed me hungrily and pulled me down on top of her. Soon, the sights, the smells, the surroundings didn't matter.

Afterwards, I gave her the package, saying, "To prove, I love you."

Slowly and carefully, she unwrapped the velvet box and folded the paper and ribbons. When she opened the box, she cried out in delight, "A ruby. My favourite," and showered me with kisses. She handed me the chain and turned her back. Awkwardly I fumbled it on. She turned back to me, hugged as hard as she could and whispered, "Rubies are forever."

I was starting to feel paranoid in this strange place and told her to get dressed. "Let's get out of here," I said, "go to my place." Malee dressed quickly but something was bothering her.

"What is it?" I asked.

"My debt to Vithoon. I cannot stay with you until I pay what I owe."

"Screw him."

"Oh, no." She looked alarmed. "He will kill us both."

"Who is this guy?"

"A colonel in the police. He runs eight girls in Cha am, more in Hua Hin."

By this time, I was hustling her to the door but as we got to the hall a very large Thai with a dragon tattooed on his neck appeared and barred the way. He yelled something at Malee. "What's he saying?" I asked as I fingered the boat knife in my pocket. I was not going to stand a chance with this guy.

"He wants to know how much you pay."

I smiled at him. He did not smile back. "Does he speak English?"

"No."

"Okay. Tell him whatever he wants to hear."

Quick exchange in Thai. My hand was still around the knife as I wondered whether I would have time to pry out the marlin spike, before he got in the first kick.

"He wants 4000 baht," Malee told me.

I held up my left hand to reassure the guy, let go of the knife and grabbed all the bills in my pocket. I pulled them out. About 1200 baht. I gave it to Malee who passed it to the Thai.

A single, guttural command. "He wants the rest."

"That's all I've got. Tell him that."

Another brief conversation then Malee turned back to me. "He says I must give him the rest when I come back from the Butterfly Bar."

"*Sawadee*," I said and, giving him my best wai, motioned him to stand aside. To my surprise, he did, favouring me with an evil smile. When we emerged from the building, I was bathed in sweat and shaking with adrenalin.

"Who the fuck was that?" I asked.

"He works for the colonel."

We walked towards O'Doul's. I felt myself beginning to get that it's-great-to-be-alive rush that comes when a danger has passed. From experience I knew it would not last, that the adrenalin crash would bring me down. I needed a drink before that happened.

The streets were poorly lit, the road slick with rain. Must have rained while I was at Malee's place, but now the night sky was all but clear. "Look," I said and pointed to the reflection of the moon in a puddle just in front of us.

"Is good sign."

"Damned right. Now I really, really need a drink."

"But I must go to Butterfly Bar," she pleaded.

"No, that's over," I told her.

"No, no. I still owe much."

"We'll sort it out later. Don't worry about the colonel," I said with the confidence of the truly ignorant.

"He will kill us. He has to. Otherwise many of the girls from Isaan would move on to Bangkok. More money there."

"We'll work it out," I said carelessly.

"He will not care you are a Farang. He will find you."

"Don't worry," I said. "Be happy." I reached down to kiss her then said, "We'll work out the money thing."

She took a deep breath to steady herself and said, "Okay, Logan."

We stopped in to O'Doul's and, for an hour, I distracted the ex-pats around the bar with the tale of my exploits. Behind the bar, the waitresses were making a fuss of Malee and her ruby. By the third gin-and-tonic, I had a pretty good buzz. I looked over at Jack and said, "Is there any tonic in this?"

"Just enough to ward off the malaria, sport."

Later, after I had consumed far too much booze and pot, Trent drove us to my new place. "Thanks, a lot, Trent. Really appreciate it," I said as Malee helped me out of the car.

"No worries. Can't have impaired pedestrians wandering the streets."

"No really, thanks," I said. Luckily he pulled away before I launched into the I-love-you-man routine.

Malee moved in with me the next day. Two days later Vithoon, the colonel, turned up. He obviously terrified Malee although he did not threaten either of us, not directly. In fact he came across as a world weary man of the world, which he probably was. If anything, he seemed disappointed in Malee.

"She is my best girl," he said. "I would cheerfully give you the pick of the rest.

"Malee and I are in love."

He chuckled. "Love is for children." Finally he sighed, seemingly resigned to losing her, and asked, "Did she tell you how much she owes me?"

Malee was not sure how much she owed but guessed around 200,000 baht, a little less than $8000. The colonel turned to Malee and spoke gently in Thai. I could tell by her face that she was getting upset. He turned to me and said, "The figure is actually 275 thousand. As I just told her, the funeral for her father was a great expense."

For half an hour he and I drank Mekong whisky and bartered for my bride. In the end we agreed on 245,000 baht.

Ransoming Malee had certainly been the high point of the past few weeks even though it meant my battered finances were taking another hit. The markets were continuing to fall and, along with most of the other ex-pats, I was really starting to feel it. Except on the weekends when Larry and Susan

played and the Scandies came up from Hua Hin, the atmosphere at O'Doul's had become almost funereal.

Malee and I usually sat on one of the couches or at a table.
Malee, a Thai woman, would not have been welcome on the
bar stools with the middle-aged ex-pats anyway. Jack came
over with Fon. They sat down across the table.

"Hear about Ken?" he asked.

Ken, the fat Australian who came in every few nights and
complained about everything Thai? "Yeah."

"Got wiped out in the markets. Not only that. He went up
to Bangkok for a few days to see if his embassy would help
him and his wife get to Australia. When he got back, the house
had been stripped and his Thai wife had left, pissed off back
up to Isaan. He's trying to scrounge up fare back to Oz."

"We're having a 50/50 draw for him," Fon says. "It was
Jack's idea."

"Sure," I said. "How much are people putting in?"

"Most people are pretty tapped out at the moment. Couple
of thousand baht."

I turned to Malee. "Have we got that much?"

Malee opened her purse and handed me the money. Out
of the corner of my eye, I noted the look of surprise on the
faces of both Jack and Fon.

The next morning as usual I was down at the cyber café
after breakfast and sending urgent emails off to Canada. Until
now, Greg had been stalling, telling his investors not to panic,
that their money was safe. I had been asking him to cash me
out $250,000 of my money, and to transfer it into my account
at Scotia Bank where I could access it. So far he had not got
back to me. Every day I checked and every day the amounts in
my Canadian accounts continued to trickle away alarmingly.

Once again my message to Greg went unanswered. Even though I was pretty sure that Greg had ripped everybody off, even his own grandmother, the email from the Sudbury Regional Police addressed to all shareholders came as a shock: Greg Paulsen was being charged with several fraud-related offences so if anyone had any information about his where-abouts, and so on. Other emails began to flood in telling me that the bastard had disappeared and so had our money. The bitter email from my sister blaming me for getting her involved with Paulsen really stung.

Even though part of me had expected this news, I sat stunned, staring at the messages of anger, grief, and fear that were flooding my in-box. Eventually, I got up and walked out into the clinging humidity. Rainy season. Heavy cumulus clouds darkened the sky as I wandered aimlessly down to the beach, a solitary middle-aged Farang trying to surf a tsunami of bad news. The wind was picking up and the only other occu-pant of the beach was the boy selling kites. I watched as he ran parallel to the waves, trailing two of his biplane kites, their tiny propellers whirring in the wind. Seeing me, he stopped and came over. "50 baht," he said, offering me one of the little plastic kites. "Good price. You children will like."

"I don't have any children," I told him.

"No children?" He looked puzzled. "You come here to be *bikkhu*?"

I laughed for the first time in a while and, passing him my last 140 baht, took two of the kites. The little biplanes were red, white and blue, the colours of the Thai flag.

His eyes went wide and he tried to give back the forty baht. "Keep it," I said. He probably did not understand the English but the wave of my hand was enough. He tucked the money in his pocket and ran off, biplanes whirring behind him. The rain suddenly exploded from the sky without warning, sheets blowing across the beach. I was soaked in seconds but still stood there watching the boy. A monk?

My thoughts turned to Malee. How was I going to break the news to her and, more important, how would she react to being broke. Over the last few days I had heard several tales of Thai wives disappearing when the bad news hit.

At the door, she greeted me with a cold beer. I thanked her, but when she hugged me the tension in my body let her know that something had happened, something bad.

When I told her that the money had gone, she smiled at me. First time she had smiled over tragedy was when she told me about her father dying. At that time, her reaction puzzled me until I asked Fon about it. "She doesn't want you to be sad for her," Fon had explained. "It's a Thai way of being."

When I finished with "So that's it, *tilak*, no money", she flung her arms around my neck and said, "We'll be all right, you'll see." I felt the wetness of her tears on my neck contradicting her broad smile.

"No wedding," I said. Might as well get all the bad news out at once. We had been planning to go north to her village in Isaan and have a Buddhist ceremony.

"Is okay."

"I'll get some money together." I thought of asking Trent but, so far, I had too much pride for that. So far.

"I can work," she said softly.

"Let's see what I can come up with first," I told her quickly. "At least the house is paid for."

The evening found us at O'Doul's and, after supper, I moved up to the boys at the bar and poured my trickle of grief into the general pool of unhappiness. The other guys made sympathetic noises. About an hour later, Sean and his *katoey* joined us. Both were red-eyed.

"What's up?" one of the ex-pats asked.

"You guys hear about Rex?" When we stared at him blankly, he said, "The poor man shot himself, so he did."

Reactions of surprise and dismay were followed by demands for more details. "I don't know if you know he always carried a Colt Commander," said Sean.

"The 45 automatic he was so proud of?" someone chimed in.

"Yes, that's what he used. His wife, her name's Sunisa, I think. She found him," Sean said.

Jack said, "You know I…" but that is as far as he got because the patio suddenly filled with the roar of a large machine.

"It's Billy with his new Harley," someone yelled and we all looked towards the open wrought iron gates that marked the entrance to the patio. Sure enough, there was Billy cranking the throttle open one last time, before shutting the bike off and dismounting.

All the guys drifted from the bar to the entrance.

Right on cue, Sean asked, "What kind of bike is it?"

"It's a Harley," someone else pointed out as if Sean was an idiot.

"I prefer vehicles with at least two more wheels," said Sean, not at all put out.

"Is that Neville's bike?" I asked.

"His pride and joy," agreed Billy. "He's got one kid…"

"The boy who likes to play on the bike."

"Right. And his wife's got another bun in the oven. He needed something more practical like my old Nissan."

"Nice machine," said Jack.

"Nice machine?" said Billy, taking centre stage. "Gentlemen, you're looking at a Harley Fatboy. 1455 cc's of power. Greatest road bike every made."

Trying to look clever, I bent down and checked the rad just behind the front wheel. "Air cooled?"

"Yeah, and she's got alloy wheels, dual pipes. Here listen." He started her and let her idle. The bike produced a throaty, irregular idle that sounded as if it was constantly on the point of stalling. "That's the Harley sound, right there," Billy pointed out proudly. "Those Jap pieces of shit idle a lot faster and they don't have that base note."

"Sweet," Jack said.

"Great wheels," I told him.

For a while, we all tried to sound like we knew motorcycles but it was not long before we ran out of things to say.

"What's the chance of a ride then," Sean said.

"Can't. Look. The Fatboy only comes with one seat."

"Ah, yes, I see."

"Here's a factoid you'll like though, Sean," Billy offered. He had become famous for his factoids, usually obscure pieces of trivia he probably got off the net. "See the colours."

"Yellow and black," I said so he could finish.

"Yeah, pearl yellow and black. These are the colours of the original bikes."

"Right."

But Billy was not finished. "Same reason they were called Fatboys. See when Harley refinanced in the early 90's after the Nips almost bankrupted them, this is the bike they brought out. Fatboy was the name of the atom bomb we dropped on Hiroshima. And the bomb was painted yellow and black."

"No shit!" said Jack.

"You can look it up," said Billy as he always did when he dropped one of his factoids on us. He swung his leg over the saddle as the crowd drifted back into O'Doul's. I was the last to leave. "Hear you're money's gone down the toilet, Logan."

"Yeah."

"Look, meet me for breakfast tomorrow. Got a deal you might be interested in."

"Okay." What did I have to lose?

He nodded, "You know bikes?"

"Not really. Crashed a couple, still got the scars."

"Pity, but I figure you know how to handle yourself."

"Been in a couple of scraps. Why?"

"We'll talk at breakfast."

"Does it involve money?"

"Oh, yeah," he said. He dropped the Harley into gear, swung her head around and headed back towards his place.

When I arrived at Neise's for breakfast the next morning, I was surprised to see Billy's Fatboy already parked at the curb. We both ordered the Aussie breakfast and when Neville brought the coffee Billy launched right in: "Sounds like you got pretty much wiped out by that son of a bitch."

"Yeah. Pretty much. How're your finances holding up?"

"Not so great. Day after I bought the Fatboy, my so-called financial advisor back home tells me the deals he had set up for me were all going sour. Still got a few bucks under my mattress but I gotta tell ya, I'm hurtin'."

"Yeah. I know the feeling." I sipped my coffee impatiently waiting to hear about the deal.

"Had to stop work on the reno to my bar. And I can't sell it until I finish the inside."

"Yeah." Breakfast arrived.

"Now I know you're pretty strapped right now so I'm thinking you might be up for a little ride to Cambodia."

"Cambodia?"

"Yeah." He looked around but at this early hour most of the tables were still empty. Nevertheless, he whispered, "It's worth just under twenty-five thou a piece, U.S. dollars. Interested?"

No way was this going to be legal. "I'd need to know the deal first. I don't want to end up in a Cambodian cell."

He laughed. "Not a chance, man. The deal is already set up."

"Who else knows about it?" I noticed I was not saying "no."

Billy pushed away his plate, signaled for a beer and lit a cigarette. I was not hungry any more either and decided on a breakfast beer too. "Let's go down to the beach," Billy said. "More private. I'll get the bill."

"What about the beers?"

"Take them with us."

Twenty minutes later we were sitting under a shade tree sipping beer and watching the tide curling in. "So what's the deal, yaa baa?"

"No money in yaa baa. Heroin."

"Jesus! Are you crazy?"

"No, no, no, hear me out. You want to know why it'll work?" Pause for effect. "Because the Thai cops are setting it up."

"What cops?"

"A colonel, smart dresser, out of Hua Hin."

"Vithoon?"

"Bingo. You know him?"

"You might say. I had to pay Malee's debts to him."

Billy started to laugh. "So he's like your father-in-law. Small world."

"And you trust him?"

"Rex did a run for him about a year ago. Worked out fine. Unfortunately Rex is no longer for hire so he came to me. My wife is a relative of his. Don't worry. He won't screw us over."

"So, you interested?"

Tempted, but scared to death and more than a little antsy about getting involved in the heroin trade. "If it was pot or even yaa baa, I wouldn't have any problem but heroin? That's heavy stuff."

Billy laughed and said, "Ever look up the side effects of heroin? Sure it's addictive and, if you shoot too much, you can OD but the rest is euphoria and wild dreams." I could feel one of Billy's factoids coming on. "Look, I'll just give you one example of a legal drug that is way more dangerous."

"Okay." I leaned forward knowing from experience that Billy liked an attentive audience.

"Ever heard of a drug called Abilify?"

"Doesn't ring a bell," I admitted.

"You've seen ads for it on TV. Abilify is a drug that you're supposed to take to make your antidepressants work better. Ever seen the list of side effects?" I shook my head. He looked up at the trees and I could see he was trying to recall what he had read on the net. He began checking off the symptoms on his fingers as he talked, "How about this...vomiting, convulsions, loss of bladder control, impaired motor responses, loss of consciousness.... The list goes on and on but you get the idea. Those bastard drug companies can advertise their shit on TV while they make sure the drugs they haven't patented are illegal. You can bet that if one of the drug companies had a patent on smack, you'd be seeing ads for it on CNN."

"Yeah, you've got a point."

"Nobody ever had to advertise heroin. People will beat down your door."

"True enough," I conceded, and then added, "Is that true about Abilify?"

"You can look it up," Billie said.

We both stared at the waves curling in for a while until I said finally, "How long will it take?"

"Couple of days, three at the most. Less than three hundred and fifty miles. No more than forty or fifty miles once we cross the border."

I looked across the bay. Just visible through the haze, the high rise pleasure palaces of Hua Hin.

"How're we getting there?"

"On my new machine."

"Your Harley? It doesn't have a rear seat."

"Right. We'll put one on. Look."

Billy pulled a creased picture out of his wallet, a picture out of some brochure of the optional rear seat. He handed it to me.

"Doesn't look very comfortable," I objected.

"You can buy a lot of painkillers for twenty-five stacks." True.

"I don't know where I could get the factory-made seat but you know the Thais. They can fake anything. You know that place next to O'Doul's?"

"The place where all they seem to do is play cards and eat noodles?"

"They also fix stuff. That's their business. I'll show them the picture and they'll build us a rear seat in a couple of days. The rear pegs are already on the bike."

"And the trip's only three days?"

"No more than four."

And twenty-five grand. A lifeline to a drowning man. Mind you, I didn't believe for a minute that Billy was splitting the take down the middle but it was his gig. And twenty-five grand. Then it struck me: "Why do you need me at all?"

"You've seen the rest of these assholes. I need someone to cover my back and you're the only guy around here I figure can handle himself. You got a gun?"

"No."

"Can you handle one?"

"Hey, I used to hunt and I'm a fair shot. I prefer a knife." I showed him the boat knife with its sharp blade, marlin spike and shackle wrench. "This will do me. If this job needs guns, I'm out."

"Don't worry, I'll take care of it. The colonel's lending me a Glock."

I let a long silence gather as I lay back on the beach grass and looked up into the trees. Three days. "What about the border?" I asked, sitting up.

"The colonel's set that up. Hey, we can even renew our visas on the way back into Thailand."

I took a deep breath, hoping I was doing the right thing. "Yeah, okay, I'm in."

We shook hands on the deal. "Beer. I'm buying," he said as we got up and brushed the sand off our asses. As we walked along the beach road, he noticed that I was carrying not only my empty beer bottle but his as well. "Taking them back for the deposit?" He laughed again.

"I draw the line at littering. Everybody's got something."

Billy roared with laughter. "Jesus! You Canucks are some cheap bastards!"

Turned out altering the Fatboy took a full week. "They ran into a problem disconnecting one of the pipes on each side," Billy explained. "Should be ready to leave in a couple of days."

"I thought they were just putting on a back seat. What's with the exhaust pipes?" I asked, pretty sure I had figured out the answer.

"More cargo capacity," he said with a grin.

By the fourth day, I was so edgy that Trent suggested we get out of town for the day, go to Wat Huay Mongkol.

"It'll be just like old times," Trent said when I jumped in his car. Malee waved goodbye from the garden. As we pulled away, I realized that I had fallen into the pattern of the other ex-pats who always seemed to leave their women at home. Still, she was busy setting up the spirit house in our garden, making sure it would be high enough to avoid the shadow of the house falling on it during the course of the day, which would cause bad luck, and low enough that she could easily reach it with the daily offerings. As I looked back, the astrologer we had hired was talking earnestly to her.

"How's the astrologer working out?" Trent asked.

"What? Oh, okay, I guess. Malee seems to like him."

"Can't be too careful. This land is full of spirits." I looked over to see if he was kidding. "When's the house warming?" he asked, meaning the party to initiate the spirit house.

"Right after I get back from Cambodia. I told Malee that there was no way we could afford it before then."

"A little soon to renew your visa, isn't it?" That was the story Billy and I had put around. "Didn't they give you the full year deal for retiring here?"

"Yeah, but…" And then I knew I had no choice but to tell him about the deal.

"So it's all about the money," he said when I had finished.

"Yeah. Reeks of desperation, I know."

"I doubt if the border will be a problem, not if Vithoon has set it up. He's a ruthless bastard though. Don't trust him."

"Oh, I won't."

"What if I told you I'd lend you the money until you got on your feet?"

"Neither a borrower nor a lender be," I quoted. "Shakespeare was right. Quickest way to kill a friendship." Over the past few weeks I had noticed a change in Trent since his huge inheritance, a change I had not anticipated. Now that people knew he had money, he had received many requests for loans or gifts. He had become paranoid that people only sought him out for his money. No way I wanted him to think I was ready to join that crowd.

"Okay, but I'll keep the offer open."

"Thanks, Trent. I appreciate it." And I did.

Wat Huay Mongkol was dominated by a giant black granite statue, not of the Buddha, but of Thailand's most famous monk, Luang Pu Thuat. The wat was set in beautiful grounds with rivers, gardens and pavilions. As we made our donations and were given offerings in exchange, I said, "We're the only westerners here."

"Yeah. Isn't it great? I'd be willing to bet that not one of the ex-pats in Cha am has ever been here."

We stopped in front of a large wooden elephant sporting three raised trunks and watched the Thais circling under the belly of the statue and the upraised trunks for good luck.

I looked up at the statue. Luang Pu's dark eyes seemed to be staring at me from under his overhanging brows and for the first time since deciding on the ride to Cambodia, I felt the ever present knot in my stomach relax.

Trent and I presented our flower offerings under the feet of the sacred monk and lit our three joss sticks. I stayed kneeling there for some time feeling a great stillness that seemed to emanate from the monk. Later, Trent and I circled the statue and, at each of the three small Buddha shrines, we carefully unrolled a single leaf of pure gold and rubbed it on to the statues. The rest of the day, we spent wandering down by the river.

The sun was dropping towards the horizon and the colourful Thai buses were leaving before we walked back to the car. Ahead of us was a Thai family. Suddenly the small boy stooped down, picked up something and showed it to his father. The father looked around, saw us and said something to the boy. As we walked up, the boy greeted us and held out his hand. In his palm was a small Buddha pendant. The boy motioned for me to take it. I looked at his father who smiled and nodded. I took the pendant. The boy grinned and ran back to his parents. I gave them a wai which they returned. "Making merit," Trent observed. "Good for his karma."

"And mine," I said.

As we turned back on to the main road I told Trent, "I needed that."

"Me too. This is where I come when I need to get away from it all. I figured you would feel it too."

"Good karma."

"Good karma."

Two days later I climbed up behind Billy amid good-natured taunts from the ex-pats seeing us off outside O'Doul's. I had told Malee I hated goodbyes so she had not come. "Be careful, Logan." The soft voice came from behind me. I turned and saw Fon looking at me, a worried look on her face. As I caught her eye, she turned away.

Before I could reply, Billy dropped the Fatboy in gear and we roared off. At that moment my misgivings fell away. With the wind tearing at my hair, I leaned back and began to enjoy the Thai panorama flashing by. What could possibly go wrong?

Covered in sweat, I stared up at the ancient ceiling fan, willing it to move. It stayed still, of course. Willpower is no substitute for electricity. The fan wouldn't rotate until someone from the village got some fuel for the generator. I fingered the knife wound in my side. A slight fleshy ridge hot and painful to the touch. My busted leg was still throbbing but less than the day before yesterday when the woman and two of the men had held me down while they set the bone and tightened the splint. After that the woman gave me some water and then one of the men offered me an opium pipe. There were no other painkillers in this nameless village and certainly no antibiotics. The woman has been treating my wound with poultices of some foul smelling herbs.

Be good if I could even thank them but although I had some Thai, I was on the wrong side of the Thai/Cambodia border. These villagers probably spoke some Khmer dialect. Three bare-assed kids ran in and out of the hut and sometimes stopped to chatter at me. I would smile and say a few words in Thai hoping that they might understand. They gave no sign but the little boy, boldest of the three, ran out and returned hiding something behind his back. The two little girls giggled behind their hands as the boy proudly produced a tiny yellow rubber duck. He squeezed it and it gave a squeak. The girls doubled over in laughter at the sound. The boy took a step towards my bed, and held the toy out for me to take it. Despite the pain, I could not help smiling. His mother came in and gently guided the children out into the compound.

I slipped in and out of consciousness. The opium gave me vivid dreams. The roar of the diesel generator woke me this time and, as I watched, the ceiling fan began to circle slowly, wobbling from side to side. Dark outside now but a single kerosene lamp elbowed the shadows back into the corners of the hut. Beyond the small window just above my head, a wealth of stars glittered above the encroaching jungle. At least I could see the mosquitoes in the light. Somehow that seemed better than listening to their infernal whine in the darkness. To the villagers, the mosquitoes, the flies, the snakes and the mice were just a fact of life. With true Buddhist indifference they ignored what they could not change.

One of the little yellow lizards was perched on the window sill. I cheered him on as his tongue darted out and snagged a mosquito.

I began to nod off and, once again, I am perched on the makeshift back seat of Billy's Harley Fatboy riding down the dark track that will eventually take us out to the road back to the Thai border. Billy is high on yaa baa, the amphetamine of choice in this part of the world. The rain has just stopped and Billy is taking it easy. The Fatboy with its wide tires and low clearance was never built to leave the tarmac and even Billy realizes how goddam dangerous this dirt road is now. When we came in yesterday afternoon, the red mud had been hard, the potholes easy to spot. Now the potholes are full of water and the mud slick. We had already come off once when a water buffalo suddenly loomed up in front of us. Not for the first time, I am cursing myself for coming but I take some strange comfort from the thought that I really did not have any other choice, not since the money dried up.

We have just rounded a bend when Billy yells, "Hear that?"

I listen. Someone is coming up behind us. I glance back. Faint glare of headlights on the wet trees. Whoever it is is getting closer though. "Yeah, I hear it," I tell him.

"Don't like it. People don't travel at night in this part of the world."

I peer back again. Now I can see the headlights. A small truck maybe, probably a Toyota.

Billy opens the throttle carefully until we both feel the speed wobble starting. He slows down again. A minute later, the truck's headlights are illuminating our backs. I have a really bad feeling about this. "Maybe we should lay it down, take our chances in the jungle," I tell him.

"Not a chance." Billy will never part with the smack stuffed into the bike's frame.

The road widens a fraction and the truck surges up beside us. A white Toyota truck spattered with mud. Crammed into the small cab, three of the guys we dealt with earlier in the day.

"Grab my gun!" Billy yells, desperation in his voice.

I put one hand down to the small of his back where he keeps the Glock 9 mm but just as my fingertips find the butt, the driver of the Toyota gives us a humourless smile and jerks the truck into the bike. I feel my leg crack as the fender slams into us. The bike spins on its axis throwing me ahead down the track and then I am on the ground sliding through mud and water. The bike is somewhere behind me. When I skid to a halt, I lie still hoping they'll forget about me. All I can see is the glare of the headlights. Then a silhouette passes in front of them and disappears towards the edge of the jungle. I listen for a shot from Billy's Glock but all I hear is a single scream then silence. I drag myself towards the anonymity of the jungle. Behind me I hear voices probably speaking in Khmer. Sounds of the men grunting with effort and then a loud metallic crash. Clang of a tailgate and then truck doors slamming. The headlights approach slowly. Terrified, I try again to drag myself all the way off the slick dirt track but now the light is on me. Tremendous relief as I realize that, with great difficulty, backing and gunning the four wheel, they are turning around. Relief turns to dread as they stop with the motor running and I hear the passenger door open and someone splash into the mud. "Don't!" I say as he looms over me but then the knife flashes and there is a hot pain in my side. Wordlessly he walks back to the truck. By the glow of the taillights I see the outline of Billy's bike in the cargo box. Two minutes later the truck crests a rise and disappears. The sound gradually fades to nothing. I call Billy's name but my breath is ragged and my calls faint. At some point the rain starts again and I begin to cry over my own fate.

And I woke up here. All that was three or four days and a lifetime ago. Not exactly the new life I had planned.

Yesterday, the woman who tended to me brought an old man, very frail, to see me. He had a kindly voice but I was about to gesture that I did not understand Khmer when I realized he was not speaking Khmer but heavily accented French.

French. Why had I not thought of that? This part of the world had once been French Indochina.

My French was only passable and, I suspected, many years had passed since the old man had last used the language.

"*Mort*," he said when I asked him about Billy. I had been pretty sure but even so it hit me hard. When he had gone, I reached into my pocket and pulled out the Buddha amulet the Thai boy had given me at Wat Huey Mongol. The amulet, shaped like a tear drop, held an image of a very young Buddha seated cross-legged before a flame. I had developed a habit of pulling it out in times of trouble; for reasons I could not explain, I drew comfort from it.

The old man had motioned to the man of the house and soon the man was back with a pipe and I drifted into the nether-world of opium where nothing really hurts anymore.

When the time finally came to leave the village and head back into the world, I wept with gratitude and frustration: gratitude for these people who had saved my life and asked nothing in return; frustration because, despite roughly two months of tutoring by the old French-speaking Khmer, I had been unable to master more than a few words of the language. Nevertheless, before I climbed into the back of the water buffalo cart, I placed my hands together in front of my fore-head in a high wai of great respect and added my heartfelt thanks in my shaky Khmer, "*Âwkun, âwkun*," and my good-byes, "*Chum ree-uhp lee-uh.*"

Just before the cart started moving, the little boy darted forward and held out the rubber duck I had left on my bed. Touched, I took it and fumbled in my pocket to give him something in return. I felt my amulet and my boat knife. Nodding for him to take it, I passed him the knife.

My Khmer samaritans were still waving when the cart carrying the driver and me rounded the first corner on the muddy track and the jungle closed around us. Hours later, we reached a paved road. The old driver gestured for me to sit in the shade of a tree and pointed west towards the border. When I was seated, he gave me a toothless smile, turned the cart around and disappeared the way we had come.

I waited for what seemed like a long time, occasionally getting up and walking about when the bugs got too bad. My leg was still sore when I put weight on it but I was hoping that, given time, the pain and the limp would disappear. Eventually, a decrepit, dusty bus with a serious list to port appeared and I flagged it down. I took out a handful of riel bills that I had bought at the border on the way in. The driver nodded, squinted around the smoke from the cigarette in the corner of his mouth and took 6000 riels, about $1.50. I took a seat beside a woman with a live chicken in a plastic bag and leaned back, grateful to be heading back to Thailand.

At the border the Cambodian official gave me grief because my thirty-day visa has expired. I paid the inflated fine with the last of my riels, glad to get rid of them. On the Thai side when I handed over my passport to renew my visa, the immigration official peered at my photo and challenged, "This you picture?"

"Yes," I told him and pulled out my wallet to show him my Ontario driver's licence, credit card and a handful of other I.D. Although he still looked skeptical, he granted the visa and I moved on. Not until I was outside in the heat did I seek out a window to look at my reflection. No wonder he had been suspicious. My beard and hair were wild and unkempt. When I got to Hat Lek, the nearest town of any size on the Thai side, I was feeling exhausted and checked into a small pension before going out to buy some toilet supplies. I also picked up a couple of cheap T-shirts: a blue one with "Bangkok" in English and Thai on it and a yellow one with "Chang Beer."

After a fitful sleep, I shaved off my beard and hacked off some of my locks so that I looked a little less scary to strangers. Next a cold shower as there was no other kind and the luxury of brushing my teeth with real toothpaste. Before going out again, I checked to see how much money I had left: about 4000 baht, say $130-140 CAD. Not bad. Enough to get me back to Cha am. I also found my unused Thai phone card. In Cha am, they probably thought Billy and I were both dead. I hesitated with the card in my hand and thrust it back into my wallet. First I needed something to eat.

As the sun began to fade, I ate at a noodle stall and then found a backpacker's bar and ordered an ice-cold Singha beer that tasted like nectar after so long. Within a couple of minutes I ordered another but this time I sipped it slowly and watched the crowd of young Farangs who seemed to me now like aliens from another planet. Finally getting up enough nerve, I retreated to the dark hall leading to the washrooms and found the pay phone. Taking a deep breath, I called my place in Cha am. A couple of rings and then an unfamiliar Thai voice came on. I didn't understand the message but guessed it meant the phone had been disconnected. So what had happened to Malee?

Frantically I dug out O'Doul's number. I was half way through dialing when I realized I didn't want to talk to anyone at the bar and hung up. I called Trent's cell. He answered on the third ring.

"Hi, Trent. You alone?"

"Jesus! Yeah, I'm in my car driving into Bangkok. We thought you were dead."

"So did I. Long story. Billy is dead. Those bastards across the border killed him and..." Suddenly the pent up emotion burst out of me in a single agonizing cry despite all my defenses. My legs were suddenly weak and I had to lean on the wall holding on to the top of the old pay phone for support.

"You okay?" Trent's voice, concerned. "Hey, Logan. You okay? Where are you?"

But I still had no voice. The air I was breathing felt thick and unfamiliar. I took thick, gulping breaths, tears streaming down my face. People squeezed past. No one stopped.

Trent again. "Look, Logan. I can hear you're pretty shattered so just listen. This is important."

"Uh huh," I managed.

"Malee's sold everything and gone back up North to Isaan. She even sold the house. And most important…You listening?"

"Yeah."

"Word is the colonel is after you and Billy. He'll kill you if you show your face around here."

Despite the unrelenting bad news, I was beginning to get hold of myself. "Malee left?"

"She thought you were dead. A matter of fact, we all did. It's been nearly three months." I was silent for perhaps a minute. "Logan! You still there?"

"Yeah."

"I'll come and get you. Let me know where you are."

"Tomorrow. I'll call again tomorrow when I get my head straight."

"You need money?"

"No, no, I'm fine." He was offering a lifeline and I was turning it down. How crazy was that? Except I had promised myself never to take his money because eventually it would cost me his friendship. And Trent seemed to be the only friend I had left. "I'll… I'll just call again. No worries."

I hung up and made my way back through the bar and out onto the street.

For a while, I walked the streets, ignoring the babble of the backpackers and the smells of the night stalls. At one point a tree wrapped in white cloth loomed out of the darkness. I stopped before it trying to remember what the wrapping meant. A group of four or five Thais approached and, when they saw the tree, gave it a wide berth. Yes, of course. The white cloth meant that the tree contained a spirit, a *phi*, that must not be disturbed. Three months ago, I would have dismissed the tree and the Thais' reaction to it as merely charming, but not now. Since that awful night on the muddy track in Cambodia, my rescue by strangers, and my long convalescence, I had begun to understand and even share a little of the Buddhist view of life.

Eventually, I wandered back to my room and lay naked on my back under the mosquito netting listening to the mosquitoes' whine and watching the slow rotation of the fan by the light from the window. Afraid to fall asleep because then I would have to relive Billy's death again. Nearly three months since Billy's murder and every night in my mind he is reincarnated only to die again. And Malee? What to make of her. How would she react if she knew I was alive? I was beginning to feel like a ghost.

When the first rays of sun slid in the window, I got up, gathered my few things and headed for the tiny bus station. Quite a few people at this early hour, mostly Thais but a few backpackers heading back to Bangkok. A guy with a tricycle cart sold me a green coconut for a few baht. With a practised swing, he lopped off the top with a machete and popped a straw into the hole. Finding an unoccupied bench under a tree across the road from the bus station, I sat down and sipped the coconut milk while I tried to work out what to do.

By the time I finished the coconut milk, I had come to the inescapable conclusion that I had nowhere left to run and little left to lose. The realization felt both terrifying and liberating. In my hand was my last talisman, the Buddha amulet the boy had given to me at the wat. A flash of movement and I looked up to see another small boy running nimbly through the traffic towards me. He had something in his hand and, suddenly paranoid, I shoved the amulet into my pocket, rose and got ready to retreat. Only then did I realize that he was not interested in me. He stopped before two monks dressed in the brown robes and sandals of the forest monks. He knelt and dropped a small package into each of their begging bowls. The weight of his responsibility lifted, the boy sprang up. Only then did I notice he was wearing the same mustard-coloured Chang beer T-shirt as I was. Much bigger on him. I found myself grinning at him and pointing at my T-shirt. The boy smiled back and, on an impulse, I beckoned him over.

When he arrived, I gave him a wai and, reaching into the plastic bag that had become the sum of my luggage, I found the rubber duck and gave it to him. He squeezed it and it squeaked, to his surprise. He laughed, that pure angelic laugh that only children have, returned the wai and ran off dodging through the traffic.

Still smiling, I turned and looked for the monks. They were standing solemnly, eyes downcast in the shade of a large tree. The older monk was quite tall and, despite the bald head, the shaved eyebrows and the tan, I was sure he was a Farang, a Farang like me.

With the force of revelation it hit me all at once. The path I was seeking was the path that had been seeking me. The boys had pointed the way.

Shyly I approached the monks and asked if one of them spoke English. My guess had been right: the older one was British and had been a monk in a forest monastery north of here for sixteen years.

Urgently I told my tale, a torrent of words about the boy Buddha in my amulet, about the boy on the Harley at Neise's, the boy on the beach who had asked if I wanted to become a *bikkhu*, the boy at the wat who had given me the amulet, the Cambodian boy. And now this boy wearing the same shirt as myself had led me to the monks.

When I finally stopped, out of breath, the Thai monk whispered something to the Englishman who translated, "He says you have temple gold on your hand. He says perhaps that is a sign."

I looked down at my right hand and saw tiny gold flecks that must have been in my pocket since I had visited the temple with Trent. "From Wat Huey Mongol," I told him.

For a long time, he conversed with the Thai monk and then said to me, "Wat Huey Mongol honours Luang Pu Thuat who performed many miracles." I nodded, remembering the dark eyes that had seemed to look right into me. "Perhaps you are one of them. You really want to become a *bikkhu* and follow the eightfold path?"

"To be honest, that seems the only path still open to me."

"Then you must come with us," the British monk said simply and led the way across the street. Traffic stopped for the monks. When we reached the dusty bus, I couldn't even read the destination as the sign above the windscreen was in Thai but it did not matter any more. For the past twenty-four hours, I had felt desperation and despair but now with little money, less luggage and no prospects, I felt a surprising contentment.

Following the monks, I was about to board the bus when I realized I was still holding the coconut husk. Quickly, afraid of missing the bus, I located an overflowing rubbish container and crammed the coconut on top before weaving my way through the crowd back to the bus. No one jostled me as this was Thailand.

As I got on, I thought of the moment Billy and I decided to go on our desperate ride. "Everybody has something, Billy," I had told him. "Me, I draw the line at littering."

Billy had laughed. It was a good way to remember him.

Finding a seat across the aisle from the monks, I looked out of the window as the bus pulled out. In my pocket, I rubbed the amulet, excited for the first time in ages about the future.

That seems a lifetime ago. Not exactly the conversion of Paul on the road to Damascus, but it led me here. The sun is stronger now and begins to beat on my gleaming bald head as we file back towards the monastery bearing our brimming alms bowls. As we walk, I try to meditate on my breathing but my conversation with the abbot yesterday keeps fragmenting my mindfulness.

"Two days ago, a man came here seeking you," he told me, "a large man with a dragon tattoo on his neck."

"Vithoon's man," I said, feeling suddenly terrified. Haltingly, I began to tell my story but the abbot held up a hand and I lapsed into silence.

With a broad smile, he said, "I told him, of course, that there is no such man here."

"But..."

The abbot had motioned for silence again. "You are a *naga*, are you not?"

"Yes, Than Jao Aowaat," I acknowledged. Novices become *nagas* or snakes before they are ordained.

"Then what is the answer to the question you be asked at your ordination, the question 'Are you a human being?'"

"Ah," I said, in awe of the abbot's wisdom. "Yes, of course. Now I see. Thank you, Than Jao Aowaat."

His smooth round face had creased into a kindly smile. "Now return to your meditation."

Blue Tango

J ames ducks instinctively and pulls Sylvie down when a small
car on the other side of the four-lane highway skids out of
control and slams into the concrete divide next to their minivan. Someone in the seat behind them yells too late, "Look
out!" as the loud bang sends pieces of metal exploding over
their vehicle. Their driver barely slows down, his only reaction
a string of gallic invective directed against all other French
drivers. Sound of nervous laughter from the other passengers
as they realize the danger is past.

"You okay?" James asks. Sylvie, saying nothing, just gazes
out at the heavy traffic braking to a halt on the other side of
the barrier. She's rarely spoken since the death of their baby,
almost two months before. At first, James had thought that
he understood, that her grief had to be given time to abate,
but then came the night when he found her sitting next to the
empty crib staring at the little mobile that still circled above it.
When he tried to comfort her, she had screamed and pushed

him away. The next day, before Sylvie was up, he had put the crib in the back of their minivan and donated it, the baby clothes, the toys, the mobile and the car seat to the Salvation Army. When he got back, she was sitting at the kitchen table in her robe, staring hollow-eyed into space. By the end of the day, in desperation, he had gone online and booked this last minute trip to Paris. When he told her, she had nodded. "It'll take our mind off things," he had said.

"Yes," she had whispered.

The traffic on the other side of the freeway has stopped now. The people in the seat behind are speculating in English about how many people would miss their flights out of Charles de Gaulle Airport because of the accident. The couple squeezed into the front seat ask the driver in French if he thinks anyone has been killed. The driver shrugs. Not his business, he says.

The woman in the middle of the front seats turns around and says in French to Sylvie, "Death can happen so quickly."

"*Oui, je sais,*" Sylvie replies solemnly. A reminder of Amy? James wonders. No, no. This trip is to distract her from the pain. With difficulty, he stops himself asking Sylvie if she is okay. Nobody ever asks you that if they think you really are okay.

James and Sylvie are the last to be dropped off at their hotel, the Pavillon Opera, on the narrow rue de la tour de l'Auvergne, just a few blocks below Sacre Coeur. Their room, the concierge tells them, is overlooking the garden. The garden turns out to be a tiny, sterile courtyard and the room is gloomy and hardly big enough to turn around. When James complains and asks if they could not move to a larger room, the concierge merely shrugs and says, "There are no more rooms."

"That famous French service," James comments as the concierge leaves them alone.

Sylvie sinks onto the small double bed without even bothering to remove her shoes while he busies himself unpacking. Sylvie had always been fastidious about her clothes, proud of her fashion sense, but now when he asks if he should unpack her stuff she murmurs, "Sure." Looking around when he has finished, he finds the room oppressive and resolves to get them out to see some sights. Sylvie will feel better when they are moving. Keeping busy has been his own way of coping and, he has finally admitted to himself, a way to avoid the misery at home. Unlike James, Sylvie had taken bereavement leave. Three weeks after the baby's death he had asked her when she was going back to work. She had just stared at him, large tears welling up.

"I loved her too," he had said finally, "but life goes on. Things will never get any better sitting around here all day with the curtains closed."

Silence.

James consults the map by the light coming in the window. First stop: Sacre Coeur, he decides. Taking a deep breath, he turns back into the room and gently rouses Sylvie.

Fifteen minutes later, they are on their way, past the local *boulangerie*, up rue Rodier and across rue Condorcet. Sylvie even smiles when they meet an old man carrying two baguettes who tips his hat to her as he passes. She is making an effort, James tells himself. As they reach the top of the street, they have to stand aside on the narrow sidewalk to allow a tall North African woman to pass them. She is pushing a double stroller holding two white children. Sylvie looks at the children and her breathing becomes rapid with emotion. James takes her arm and leads her to the corner. Ahead of them, across the road is a park, the air filled with the shouts and laughter of children. Through the wrought-iron railings, James can see the children playing. Determined, he starts across the road when the walk sign illuminates, but he is alone. He turns back. Sylvie, head bowed, is turned away from him. Angry, he makes his way back to her.

"What is it?" he asks, more sharply than he had intended.

"I want to go back to the hotel, James."

He shakes his head in exasperation. "The world is full of children," he tells her, then, taking her arm, he adds, "Come on."

Sylvie wrenches her arm away and wraps both arms around a metal light standard. People passing by are casting surreptitious glances their way.

For several moments, James can only stare at her in disbelief. Finally, he says, "Okay. Why don't you go back and hide your head under the covers. The keys at the front desk."

He turns away from her, crosses the street without looking back, opens the gate into the park and walks briskly along the gravel path, past the women sitting on the benches, through the children running after each other and on, past the ancient carousel where yet more children ride on blue horses and up, up the steps through the crowds and musicians until he reaches the cool, dark confines of Sacre Coeur. Out of breath, his shirt plastered to his back with sweat, he sinks on to one of the pews. In better times, they would have been taking Amy to the park, shot pictures of her on the carousel.... What now? The children had also reminded him of Amy, of the picture that kept appearing in his head of the paramedics carrying her lifeless form down the hallway. But, dammit, life goes on. You pick yourself up and you go on. You don't keep fingering the scar. Here in the quiet of the cathedral, James admits to himself that he does not know how much longer he can stay

with Sylvie and watch as she picks at the scab of their loss.
Listening to the whispering of prayers, he wonders, not for the
first time, what life without Sylvie would be like. The thought
has come unbidden but the idea is alluring enough to make
him feel guilty even to have considered it.

When he finds his way back to the hotel, he hesitates on
the opposite corner and looks at the baguettes stacked on the
counter just inside the door of the *boulangerie*. In the window
is a pile of meringues in delicate pink swirls. He remembers
that Sylvie likes them. The woman puts two in a small paper
sack and gives him a larger bag for the baguette that he has
bought on impulse. Sylvie almost certainly has not eaten
anything.

When he comes out into the late afternoon sunlight, he
still cannot decide to go into the hotel. Not because Sylvie is
there, but because she might not be.

A motorcycle delivering sushi roars past before he can
cross to the small brasserie on the opposite side of rue Rodier
and sit at one of the outdoor tables on the sidewalk. When the
waiter comes, he orders a *bière pression*, a draft beer.

"*Sieze soixante-quatre?*" asks the waiter, smiling. When
James gives him a puzzled look, he switches to heavily-ac-
cented English and says, "It is how the beer is called."

"*Ah, mais oui, sieze soixante-quatre,*" James agrees.

While he sips his beer, James watches the passing parade
of Parisian life: the tall woman with the old french bulldog
following her up the street, the steady stream of local people
emerging from the *boulangerie*, each with two small baguettes
in a paper bag under an arm. Some enter the brasserie and
emerge clutching packs of cigarettes. More dogs than he would
have expected and they all seem to be unneutered males. Only

the smallest of dogs seems to require a leash. The rest follow their owners, stopping obediently for the traffic before crossing, waiting patiently outside the *boulangerie*. A little way up the hill leading back to Sacre Coeur is a patch of wall next to a hairdresser's that every dog stops at, sniffs and adds another note of pee-mail. This is why I came, James acknowledges, to sit at a tiny round table on a Parisian sidewalk, sip a beer in the late afternoon sunlight and breathe in the atmosphere. Only Sylvie is missing. In his mind's eye, he has seen them sitting here together enjoying the passing scene, pointing out the truck that is blocking the narrow street while the driver without hurrying unloads a few small boxes, or the father carrying a small child sleeping so soundly she is limp as a rag doll.

James signals the waiter for another beer. While he waits, he glances past the local couple who have sat down two tables from him, towards the entrance of his hotel. Because he is on the same side of the street, he can only see the sidewalk in front of it where two of the hotel staff are standing idly, smoking cigarettes. No sign of Sylvie. But then, in a way, she has been missing since Amy's death. Walk away or hang on? He has no answer.

The waiter brings him another beer and tucks the bill under the beer mat.

Is she in the room? She is either there or not there. Schrödinger's cat. As long as he does not open the box the cat is both alive and dead. As long as James sits here, Sylvie is both in their room and not. Which reality does he want to uncover? A moment of hesitation…then he realizes that he wants her to be there. This is the trip that was going to heal their marriage. Not much of a start but too early to give up yet.

He finishes the second beer, goes into the bar and pays the tab. The room number? he asks himself as he reaches the door to the hotel. Ah, 34, *trente-quatre*. The concierge is arguing with someone on the telephone. James is about to ask for the key when he realizes that if Sylvie is in the room, she will have it. Gingerly, he steps into the tiny, ancient lift and presses the button for the second floor. The cage lurches and then begins to ascend, creaking alarmingly as it passes the *premier étage*, second floor in Canada, and halts at the next gate. He lets himself out and proceeds down the narrow, poorly-lit hall to the room. Tentatively, he knocks. Nothing. He knocks again and listens at the door. Nothing. "Sylvie," he calls softly and then louder, "Sylvie!" A door opens down the hall and a bald man in a robe says something rapidly in French, too rapidly for James to catch although the body language is clear. He nods at the man, mutters "*pardon*" and retreats down the hall to the lift.

Back at the desk, he asks the concierge for the key to "*numero trente-quatre*." The concierge throws it on the counter with ill grace. Of course, she's not in the room or the key would not be at the desk. But he has to check. His stomach churning with fear, he takes the stairs up two at a time, puts the key in the door and flings it open. The bed is still made, the suitcases on the rack, his book, *Les Miserables*, still lying on the tiny bedside table. Closing the door, he crosses to the window and looks out. Below him is the arid white courtyard, misnamed "*le jardin*" in the hotel brochure.

The emptiness of the room is a relief in a way. He needs to find her but at least she hasn't.... He tries to erase the vision of her lifeless body collapsed across the tiles of the tiny bathroom floor, the vision that had spurred him up the stairs.

Carefully he examines the room before deciding that she had not returned after they had parted. He sits down at the vanity and catches a glimpse of himself in the mirror. "We'll always have Paris," he tells his reflection and then tosses the bag with the meringues and the baguette across the bed into a dark corner. "Christ!... Okay, okay, where would she have gone?" Normally he would call her cell but they have left their phones in Canada because they will not work with the European protocol.

Slowly it dawns on him: St. Sulpice. Before they'd left home he had pointed out St. Sulpice in the guidebook and told her that if they ever became separated to head for St. Sulpice. "You remember," he told her, "that church in *The Da Vinci Code* where the albino monk murdered the nun." He had shown her where it was and even copied the address into her wallet. He gets up and begins to rummage through his carry-on shoulder bag. Finding the guide book and maps, he pulls them out, turns on the overhead light and carries them over to the vanity. There it is circled on the map. On the Left Bank, too far to walk. He checks for the nearest metro station to his hotel. Up towards Sacre Coeur is Anvers but it would be better to go down rue de la tour d'Anvers to Cadet, catch a metro there and change at Gare de l'Est to route four in the direction of Porte d'Orleans. This would take him under the Seine to St. Sulpice station, a short walk from the church. He checks his watch: 19:23 local time, 1:23 in the morning on his own biological clock.

At the desk, he is about to ask if the attendant has seen his wife but a new man is on duty. The concierge pulls his attention away from a small TV long enough to take his key and offer an insincere "*bonsoir*" as James leaves.

As the Metro pulls into the Gare de l'Est station and stops, the subway door does not open. A moment of panic before a woman sitting on one of the tip-up chairs next to the door, reaches over and flips up the handle. The door opens and he directs a heartfelt "*merci beaucoup*" at her as he steps out onto the platform. Following the signs to *ligne quatre*, he manages a smile at his faux pas with the door; he remembers that he had made exactly the same mistake the first time he was in Paris, what was it, eight, no nine years ago. He had been studying in England then and had come over with Rosie for what the English called a "dirty weekend." Lots of laughs, Rosie. She had got a job at one of those universities in the southern states. Their affair had been over before she left London but they had remained friendly enough that he had seen her off at Heathrow. For a while they had emailed but gradually the correspondence petered out as such things do. Funny lady, though. Wonder if she's still married?

At the Chateau d'Eau station a young man with a shock of red hair and an armful of gear enters the car as the doors begin to close. Reaching back, he grabs a small boy and pulls him aboard. Curious, James watches the man erect a blue blanket full of stars across the aisle at the end of the car. The man disappears behind the curtain and seconds later music from a boom box fills the air and two puppets appear above the blanket. Most of the other passengers ignore the interruption but James finds himself smiling at the grinning puppets dancing above the blue blanket with its faded stars. When the train begins to slow down for the next station, the puppeteer finishes the show, drops the blanket and the child runs through the car with a hat. James drops in a one euro coin. The puppeteer and his boy get off. James wonders what Sylvie's reaction would have been.

When he emerges above ground at St. Sulpice station, he consults the map. The route to the cathedral leads him down a side street to a park opposite a police headquarters. A hand lettered sign over the entrance to the park proclaims "Marché de la poesie." A poetry market? He looks at the map again. Sure enough. St. Sulpice lies at the far side of the little park. Sylvie must have come this way if she is here at all. James feels himself getting annoyed again. She could have left him a note at the hotel desk. Surely she wasn't too grief stricken for that.

A light rain begins to fall while he is threading his way through the canvas stalls and book displays. Above the awnings he catches glimpses of the unmatched twin towers atop the façade of St. Sulpice and is suddenly reluctant to enter. For a time he wanders among the stalls looking at the offerings of earnest, unfamiliar poets, nearly all dressed in black and smoking cigarettes furiously.

Overcoming his reluctance, James starts up the steps, past a pair of nuns in black and white habits collecting for foreign missions. Ignoring their soft appeals, he enters the church. Surprisingly few people here.

No sign of Sylvie. A mass is going on with a scattering of people in attendance. He walks slowly up the side aisle scanning the faces for Sylvie's but does not see her. James had thought he might find her kneeling here, even though, like him, Sylvie is an ex-catholic.

Gleaming a dull gold, a brass strip set in the floor traverses the "cathedral of the left bank" at an slight angle in front of the main altar. The gnomon. Despite his anxiety, James feels a twinge of excitement at spotting the rose line, once intended to be 00 degrees longitude. It runs north/south through the church, the brass strip that the assassin, Silas, had followed in

Brown's book. James' eyes followed the line under the chairs set out for the congregation into the darkness beyond the high altar. Skirting the chairs, he follows the line and sees a female figure sitting on a chair beside the obelisk at the end of the gnomon. Hovering over her is one of the nuns in a black and white habit. As he approaches, he can hear Sylvie and the nun whispering in French. The nun sees him first, makes a sign of the cross as if an evil spirit were approaching. When he is a few paces away, the nun, her habit flapping, walks off quickly into the gloom behind the altar towards the Chapel of the Virgin.

Sylvie sits quietly weeping, her head bowed so she does not see him until he puts his hands on her shoulders from behind. She starts in panic. "It's me," he says softly but she rises and turns on him, her eyes wild.

For a second she stares at him as if she does not recognize him and then her features soften and she whispers his name and lets him hold her. They stand so for what seems to James like an eternity as the mass drones on behind them. Finally she looks up at him, her face pale and, still in French, tells him, "It was God's will."

The nun has been pouring poison in her ear, he decides. That's all they need. He wonders if Sylvie had confessed the abortion when she had been a child of sixteen. Of course she had. He suppresses his anger at her and says in English, "Are you okay?"

"Amy died because of my sinful life," she continues in French.

"Speak English, Sylvie," he implores her. He wants to distance her from the judgement of the nun who has melted into the shadows. "Come on. Let's get out of here." He leads her out a side door into a courtyard and they follow the side of the church until they pass the massive colonnade and thread their way back through the garden of the poets. As they emerge on rue Bonaparte, James stops and turns to face Sylvie. "It was nobody's fault. Crib death. No one really knows why it happens. You are not to blame.... You understand?" Sylvie stares at him, saying nothing. "God damn it! Don't do this to us. Do you understand?" Sylvie gives a slight nod. James smiles at her. "Nuns always gave me the creeps. Besides, neither of us is even Catholic. Right?"

Sylvie hesitates and then nods again and attempts a wan smile. "Not much of a holiday," she says in English.

James smiles at her broadly, "We'll be fine beginning now. I think I remember the way from here to Les Deux Magots." She looks at him, puzzled now. "It's a famous bar where Hemingway, Fitzgerald, all that crowd hung out in the thirties."

All the outside tables are taken, mostly by tourists, but these days even the French prefer to sit outside since the new smoking laws went into effect. The place looks much more upscale than he remembers. On the sidewalk beside the bar is an ancient black Citroen sitting on its roof, lights blazing from inside the cab. They stop to look. And then she peers in the window of the store next to Les Deux Magots and whispers, "Luis Vuitton. Look." She is pointing at the gold letters above the window. "Luis Vuitton." James is so pleased that if it had not been closed he would have taken her in to buy something, something extravagant they couldn't afford. They stroll down to the Seine past the Académie des Beaux Arts. After a *café au lait* at a small brasserie across the road from the river, they walk along the Seine in the warm evening air. Even after ten o'clock there is still light in the western sky. When they reach le pont de l'Alma, they stop for a moment. Suddenly they are

bathed in white light. Surprised they turn and find themselves
staring into a bank of parabolic lights as a tour boat illuminates
the left bank, the harsh beams streaming up at them through
the trees. Impulsively, James puts his arm around Sylvie and
leans over to kiss her. At first she resists. "It's the law in Paris,"
he whispers and she softens. Afterward, hand in hand they
walk away from the river to find the nearest Metro station.

The next day at breakfast, Sylvie seems more animated.
Although she is still looking fragile, James is pleased to see her
eat not one but two croissants with her *café au lait*. "Where are
we going today?" she asks him a little too brightly.

"Wherever you want," he tells her. "Today Paris belongs
to us."

"You choose then," she tells him. "Be my guide. Don't
forget I haven't been here before."

James nods and smiles. After the encounter with the nun,
he resolves to stay clear of the famous churches and the almost
equally famous cemeteries. He holds up three fingers. "*La
Tour Eiffel, le Louvre, ou le Bon Marché*."

"*Le Bon Marché*?"

"It's a place I think you'll like. After you fell asleep last
night, I looked through our guidebooks. When I came across
Le Bon Marché. I thought, 'That's a place that Sylvie wouldn't
want to miss.'"

"But what is it?"

"Let's just say, we'd better dress up a little when we go there."

"I don't want to go anywhere too crowded."

"So you want door number three?" She nods. To him this
morning, she has the kind of radiance that you sometimes see
in the painted faces of saints. He takes her hand. Cold to the
touch. "Then we'll go to le Bon Marché."

Two hours later they are gliding up the glass escalators and wandering around the elegant white décor of the store designed by Auguste Eiffel. The hats delight Sylvie more than anything else. James encourages her as she tries on one amazing confection after another and parades in front of the mirror. A thin woman dressed in the tailored black and white uniform of le Bon Marché, approaches and, with a frosty smile, offers assistance. When Sylvie compliments the hats in fluent French, the woman visibly softens and offers to bring more examples. For half an hour, James watches Sylvie laughing, charming the sales rep, catching the eyes of more than one husband passing by. When Sylvie finally thanks the woman who has been helping her, the woman tells her to wait. Sylvie looks at James in the mirror. He nods. The woman disappears and emerges a minute later with a small red hat made of spiralling red feathers with a brief veil. Sylvie gasps in delight and puts it on. The woman fusses with her dark hair until the hat sits perfectly. "What do you think?" Sylvie asks James.

"It is beautiful. And so are you." He turns to the saleswoman. "We'll take it," he tells her.

"Oh, no, no," Sylvie tells him, carefully removing the hat and fumbling for the price tag. "My God! It's three hundred and twenty-five euros."

"We'll take it," James insists, gently taking the hat from her. It weighs almost nothing.

"Where will I wear it?" Sylvie asks.

"Oh, I think we can find somewhere," he tells her mysteriously.

After lunch, they go back to their hotel to rest. "Where are we going tonight?" Sylvie asks as she carefully props her hat before the mirror so that she can see it from the bed.

"We'll have a good meal and then I'm taking my love dancing," he tells her. "Remember how good we were getting?"

"Yes, but that was before…"

He puts his finger to her lips. "You used to love to dance. Time to reclaim it."

"But we're not in practice."

"We're not in practice for a lot of things," he says, and, very tentatively, leans over the bed and kisses her softly.

"I'm sorry," she says, cradling his face in her hands.

"No need, my love." He slips in beside her and for the first time since Amy had left them, Sylvie and James take the chance of creating another child.

That night, following an exquisite meal near the Trocadero, they catch the metro back to Place de la Bastille. James takes Sylvie to Le Balajo, a place he and Rosie had stumbled upon his first time in Paris. Tucked up a side street, Le Balajo is a throwback to the thirties; a small dance hall where you can still dance to live music. Just inside the door is the ticket booth. While the couple ahead of them is buying their tickets, James peers down the hallway, past the brightly-lit bar and into the timeless hall. Nothing seems to have changed. James even recognizes the ancient ticket seller as he pays the twenty euros admission. The tiny stage is surrounded by cartoon skyscrapers with lights in the windows. The ceiling recedes into midnight blue studded with stars.

"It's marvellous," says Sylvie, "like stepping into the past."

One thing that has changed, James realizes, is the clarity. When he had been here with Rosie, the air had been murky with cigarette smoke that swirled in the beams of light. Now that even the French have to smoke outside, the shafts of light are invisible, the dancing couples in crisp focus.

Apart from that, Sylvie was right, they had stepped into the past, the past before Amy, hopes James, the past when Sylvie had been happy. They claim one of the booths that line the dance floor two deep and hold hands as they watch the other dancers. In turn they are watched surreptitiously by some of the other patrons. A couple of the women smile at Sylvie. Sylvie is wearing her new hat. On stage a tiny woman is singing "La vie en rose" backed up by an accordion played by an old musician dressed all in black. The only concession to modernity, the beat box that the musician tweaks occasionally.

"What did the ticket guy say when I paid him?" James asks Sylvie.

"We get a free drink with the tickets."

"Better and better. I'll be back."

Returning with the drinks, James stops just inside the door and looks at Sylvie. She has never looked more beautiful, he thinks. In the past few weeks, she has lost weight but in the ambient light of the club, her pallor and thin frame clad in the red and white dress with the handkerchief hemline make her look as elegant as anyone in the room. And the hat is perfect.

"Look at that couple," Sylvie says as he sits down and sips his beer. The singer is intoning "Yesterday When I was Young" to a slow foxtrot. James looks out at the couples circling the floor. She does not have to tell him which couple she is talking about. Both dressed in black, they are dancing almost stationary just in front of the stage. They are so closely intertwined as to be almost one. The man, much taller than the woman, has close-cropped black hair carefully slicked down. He is staring off into the darkness, carefully cradling his partner. The woman's face is invisible, pressed into his shoulder. Black sequins glitter on her dress as the lights catch them.

The next song is a rhumba. "Come on," James says.

They are tentative at first but within a few bars, the rhythms take them and they are dancing under the ceiling stars and the magical windows of the keystoned skyscrapers. After the rhumba the musicians take a break and the floor begins to clear. Last to leave the floor are the dancers in black. The man separates from the woman and kisses her hand. For the first time, they can see her face. It is slightly pulled down on one side so that when she smiles up at her partner, only the muscles on the left side move. He smiles back at her and leads her slowly off to a table next to the stage, ignoring her shuffling steps.

"Oh," says James before he can stop himself. He remembers them from his last trip to Le Balajo. They had dressed in black then too, but then they had both been superb dancers. She must have suffered a stroke. He goes to tell Sylvie but decides, at the last moment, not to. Voicing his emotion will only bring him to tears, the last thing Sylvie needs this night.

Throughout the evening, James watches as the couple in black dance rhumbas, mambos, and even the tango. James and Sylvie sit after a lively cha-cha just as the first strains of "La Cumparsita" begin. "That couple is dancing again," says Sylvie. James nods and watches. The man holds his partner close and executes *la salida*, the opening tango steps. Rather than gliding across the floor and halting with the music, they execute the move in place. The couple separates a few inches before executing a *corté* and staring fiercely into each other's eyes for a moment seeming to distill the essence of tango in one dramatic move. Sylvie reaches for James' hand across the table as they both stare transfixed at the couple. Other dancers have left an empty circle around them and smile as they dance past.

"They are wonderful," Sylvie says.

And so brave, thinks James, but can only say, "Yes."

When the strains of the "Blue Tango" begin, half an hour later, James leads Sylvie out on to the floor. "Your favourite."

"Yes."

Caught up in the passionate rhythms of the dance, they whirl through a turn, before he bends her in a dip, holds for a beat and takes her back into a rock step. Suddenly, someone is pulling at Sylvie's dress. She looks down and stops mid-step. An impossibly small child with dark eyes is offering her a rose. Sylvie crouches down and says simply, "Amy."

Amy's dead, James wants to shout. Other couples are looking at them oddly now. A couple of seconds later, the barman pushes his way through and grabs the little girl by the arm telling her to get out. He is tired of having her annoying his guests. Sylvie screams in English, "No! Leave her alone."

"Romani," the bartender says in disgust, pointing to the child as if that explained everything.

"Leave her alone," pleads Sylvie again. "Let her stay."

Many of the couples have stopped dancing and are watching the drama unfold in the middle of the floor but the musicians play on. James looks around and does not detect any sympathy for the child. Perhaps she sneaks in here frequently, perhaps similar scenes go on night after night. The bartender shrugs and begins to drag the child away. Sylvie grabs for the girl's arm but misses and ends up tumbling almost comically to the floor. The bartender and the girl disappear through the crowd. Sylvie weeps uncontrollably, sitting in the middle of the floor, gritty with dance wax. Mascara is making ugly black trails down her cheeks; at some point she has lost her hat.

Embarrassed, James pleads for her to get a grip on herself but she seems not to hear. This is it, James thinks. This is the end of our marriage right here to the last strains of the "Blue Tango." The hall goes quiet except for the sounds of Sylvie's grief. He is on the point of walking away, leaving the club and never looking back when he hears behind him a scratchy ancient voice. The tiny woman in black is bending with difficulty over Sylvie. Her lover gently supports her. In her hand is Sylvie's hat. "It looks so beautiful on you," she is telling Sylvie. The woman strokes the hat, wiping the dust and wax off the feathers and with a shaky gentleness puts it on Sylvie's head. Sylvie's sobs have subsided to an occasional sharp intake of breath. The woman takes Sylvie's hand and Sylvie rises to her feet. "You must not let your sorrows overwhelm you," the woman tells her. "The child is still part of you…"—she looks over at James—"and of your man." The woman manages a crooked smile as she strokes Sylvie's cheek. Bending closer with difficulty, she whispers something in Sylvie's ear. To James surprise, Sylvie gives the woman a grateful smile.

James thanks the woman and looks at the man in black who smiles and nods at him before proudly putting his arm around the woman and leading her slowly away. James leads Sylvie back to their table. Soon the music resumes, couples begin to dance a rhumba. Over near the bandstand, the couple in black revolve slowly to the dance.

James and Sylvie sit in silence for a while, then he feels her hand reaching for his. "I have to redo my makeup," she tells him.

"Yes," he says. As she rises, he asks what the woman in black had whispered to her.

"She told me I was carrying another child," Sylvie says.

Shaking his head in wonder, James watches her as she

crosses through the bar and disappears down the stairs to the toilets.

He sighs and looks across at the couple in black. Just for an instant, the woman catches his eye and favours him with her sad smile. James, feeling a lump in his throat, returns her smile and nods his thanks.

About the Author

Besides writing and travelling, Colin Hayward likes to sail, and has scuba dived from the Great Lakes to the Great Barrier Reef. For many years he was a professor of theatre at Cambrian College in Sudbury, Ontario, and still freelances as a director, lighting designer, actor and pyro tech. He lives outside Sudbury. In 2006 Scrivener Press published his first collection: *Other Times, Other Places: Twenty Stories.*